The Suspect

Maya Kepler

Contents

Chapter 1 ~ Sage

✱ SAGE POV *

    I lean my head against the car window and watch as the dry, vast scenery blurs together. I can hear the faint drum of my father's fingers against the driving wheel of the car as we zoom down the empty roads. I inhale deeply and look at the time displayed behind the driver's wheel and groan. We've only been driving for two hours. That means two hours since I have left my past life behind.

Moving was the last thing on my to-do list. In fact, if it were to be on any list it would be on the 'Just Don't' list. Facing the fact that I have to start all over again somewhere far far away from the place I call home makes me tremor.

My father is a detective who had just been brought onto a case about the disappearance of a 17-year-old boy in the small town of Mapleville. Because of this, I have been dragged along with him for who knows how long to live there. The thought makes me want to vomit.

Don't get me wrong, I'm thrilled for my father to have this opportunity but my life has been a constant hell ride over the past few years and things had finally felt like they were going back to normal. Well... as normal as normal could get. My mother passed away six years ago in a car accident and since then nothing has been the same. My grades went off the rails, I would shut people out and I was a disaster waiting to happen. However recently things were improving. I was back to achieving my normal grades and had mended my ruined friendships. But what good is that going to do me now?

I look at my father who is now humming away to an old song playing on the radio. 5 more hours of driving to go. How fun!

Up until now, I hadn't thought much about the disappearance of the boy. It only now occurs to me that I am going to be living in the same town and attending the same school as he attended. What if it's dangerous? What if I become a target because I am the daughter of the new detective? What if there's a murderer on the loose? I take a deep breath. I'm just being silly. I feel sure that this missing kid will turn up within a matter of time and everything will be alright and if that's not the case my Dad will get to the bottom of what happened in no time. All I need to do is blend in. There is only a year and a half of school left and then I'm free.

My stomach grumbles as I look at the open packet of gummy worms in the centre console of our car. Grabbing them, I lean back into my chair. The word free playing over and over in my mind. Oh, how sweet it sounds.

By the time we pull into our new driveway my limbs ache from sitting, unmoving and still in the cramped car. It is now dark outside, making our new house appear cold and uninviting. This is the place where I am likely to spend the rest of my schooling. That thought alone is enough to make me want to get back into the car and turn the hell around, to a place I can actually call home.

The door to our new two storied house creaks as my dad swings it open. He looks at me with an eager grin. Well at least one of us is an optimist.

I take in the wooden floors and empty space in front of me. If I'm being honest, the interior itself is quite nice, however, no amount of furniture placed in it could ever make this place feel like home.

Chapter 2 ~ Chase

C hase's POV

'He's missing.'

Those two words rocked me to the core and made my blood run cold. The person who had made my life hell was gone and nowhere to be found. Brett Reed, the golden boy of Mapleville was missing. Who would have guessed? If anyone could have escaped and done something useful with their life it was him, we weren't all as lucky as he was. We didn't all have his privileged lifestyle.

Now that I glanced around the hallway I realized something was off, there wasn't the usual chatter and laughter like there was in a typical scene from a movie. There was a silence that hung heavy in the air, making the already crowded hallway suffocating to be in.

Brett Reed. Just the thought of his name made my stomach churn with anger. How dare he disappear after what had happened and leave me here to clean up the mess. In my opinion, it was a cowardly move, considering he was the instigator.

I'm not stupid it doesn't take a genius to figure out what happens now, the hushed whispers in the hallway weren't just because Brett was missing. The whispers were about the two of us, the fight we had, and that was the last thing that happened before he went missing.

If he is trying to set me up, he was doing a good job of it. And that very thought made my frown deepen. I had a reputation. Not all of it was true, but people like to talk and embellish.

Once I reach my locker, I feel a presence to my right. I glance at him letting my eyes roam him from head to toe before I let out a grunt and turn away acknowledging the fact that the smile he was wearing falters. Good. He should honestly know better by now, I don't give anyone my time of day let alone someone who is most likely fishing for false drama.

"Chase...." he mutters now unsure of himself, the confidence he had built up had now diminished leaving him glancing back helplessly at a group of guys over his shoulder, probably his friends.

"Whoever you are, you can leave me the fuck alone."

He stares at me, mouth slightly ajar as he tries to figure out what just happened. I huff and turn to leave. I don't have time to waste on this kid. I can tell he is thinking of what to say to that, how to possibly gather more information to go back and spill to his eager friends.

"Wait I just wanted to know what your thoughts were on Brett and how he's gone, I mean do you actually believe it?"

I stop and look at him over my shoulder, who the hell was this kid, and why did he suddenly think we were friends and that I was going to give him an answer.

I turn around abruptly, catching him by surprise. I tower over his frame and I smirk, as he has to crane his neck to meet my eyes. I can see the fear slowly begin to seep in. I lean down and position myself so we are eye to eye.

He is scared, beyond scared at this point. I have an answer to the question that he doesn't look so eager to get now.

" You want to know what I think? I think you can get fucked."

And with that, I turn and walk away.

A permanent glare is embedded on my face by the time last period arrives. In fact, there are waves of anger radiating off me. I am beyond annoyed. The whispers floating around me as I sit in the tiny, dull room is claustrophobic, to say the least. Staring at the clock as my knee bounces up and down impatiently waiting for the bell. My head is swarming with thoughts overwhelming me. Brett is still gone, a part of me is waiting for him to walk through the school doors and for everything to go back to normal. But as the school day is almost over my hope for that fades.

I am the first one out of the classroom, I barge through the door, tuning out the urgent calling of my name. I keep walking. I want to escape. I need to escape.

"Chase, Chase!"

Annoyed I turn and scowl at the teacher in front of me.

"Yes," I say impatiently, just wanting to leave.

"Sorry to keep you back, but the principal has asked me to inform you that the police are here and would like to question you on the disappearance of Brett Reed."

My legs that were so ready to turn and walk out of the corridor are now routed to the spot, my mind goes blank as I mutely nod and follow her through the corridors. I had suspected this would happen but not so soon considering hes only been missing for just over 24 hours. Just because I was the last person seen with him, doesn't mean I know anymore than anyone else.

But they don't know that.

Chapter 3 ~ Sage

SAGE'S POV

one week later

I sigh. Today is the day. The day I've been dreading for the past few days. My first day at my new school.

I look at my new school uniform and slightly adjust my skirt. It's not terrible but it's not fabulous either. I gather my chestnut coloured hair in my hands and braid it. I grab an elastic, fixing my hair in place.

I make my way to the kitchen where my father is sitting eating a slice of toast. He doesn't even notice my presence, too busy fixated with some papers in his hand.

"Morning Dad," I say, giving him a fright.

"Oh, good morning sweetie. Are you excited for your first day?" He asks, turning his attention back to the papers.

"Thrilled!" I exclaim sarcastically.

"That's the spirit," he chuckles.

I grab an apple and sit down across from him. "Is that to do with the missing boy?" I ask taking a bite.

"Yes, just going over the case before I go into the office today. It's very strange," he says, muttering the last part.

Strange sounds right. From what I know (which are just basic details) the disappearance seems very odd. Brett Reed a 17-year-old wealthy boy went missing a week ago. He never returned home after school that day and no one has heard anything since.

"Well, I'm sure you'll get to the bottom of it. Now I must get going. I don't want to be late on my first day," I say, picking my school bag up.

"Have fun and make some friends!" My Dad shouts out as I make my way to the front door.

"Hmmm, I'll think about it," I shout back, slinging my bag over my shoulder.

Being the new student arriving half way through the school year is not my idea of a great start. I look at the time on my phone. 7:50 am. School doesn't start until 8:40. That means I have plenty of time to get to school, figure out where I'm going and maybe make some friends. Maybe.

My main priority is to blend in. Maple High is the only high school in Mapleville which means that everyone my age living in this town is in attendance.

When I arrive at school there are only a few students roaming around. None of them even give me a glance as I walk past them and into the school building. I'm beyond fine with that. I walk through the open door and am met with a long hallway with long lockers lined along the walls. There are a group of girls huddled in the corner and two guys over near a drinking tap. Apart from that, the hallway is deserted. Well, I guess that makes sense considering school doesn't start for another 40 minutes.

"Don't worry, it's not always this quiet," a bubbly voice says from behind me, giving me a fright. I turn around. A small girl with blonde hair and brown eyes is beaming at me. "You're Sage right? The new student? I'm Alice," she says extending her hand for me to shake.

I grab it giving a smile back. "Hey, how'd you know I was new?" I ask curiously.

"It's not a large town. It's easy to pick a newbie from a local," she smiles. "Anyways the principal asked me to show you around because we both have the same first class, literature. So why did you move here?" She asks.

"My dad is a detective and is working on a new case here to do with a disappearance," I say not letting on about how much I know in case it's being kept a secret.

"Oh, the disappearance of Brett Reed? Terrible isn't it! So bizarre as well!" She sighs, "He's Mr Popular around here. Everyone always wanted to be his friend. Well, I'm sure they still will when he returns."

"What's so good about him?" I ask.

"There are multiple things. He's head of the football team, holds the best parties, has the features of a God etc. Every girl wants to date him and every boy wants to be him. Well except for this one guy," she chuckles. "Your father will surely be a hero when he discovers what has happened to Mapleville's golden boy."

By now the hallway is bubbling with people. Alice shows me the toilets, classrooms and takes me to the office where I receive my locker number and timetable. Before I know it, it's first period and Alice and I are walking into class. I get a few odd looks but choose to ignore them as Alice begins telling me about our strict literature teacher who is known for his harsh marking and lack of humour before someone stops her and strikes up a conversation about a volleyball game.

After a minute of awkwardly standing there, I decided I may as well choose a seat. I scan the classroom looking for a place to sit. I definitely don't want to sit at the front, especially if Mr Red, our teacher, is strict. Ideally, I would prefer a middle seat but they were already taken. I look towards the back. There in the middle was a free seat. I look around to make sure no one was making their way towards it. I decide it is vacant and quickly walk to it.

I put my bag on the ground and sit in the chair. As the bell rings signalling the start of the lesson I take out my books and place them on the desk. It is only seconds later in which I notice an odd and uncomfortable silence. I look up and meet the eyes of many questioning faces.

"You probably shouldn't sit there. It's Chase River's seat," a guy with blonde hair sitting next to me whispers.

"Who's Chase Rivers?" I ask, uncertain as to why this Chase guy has his own reserved seat.

Before the blonde guy answers, I notice a looming figure approach my desk. I look up and have to prevent myself from choking on my own saliva. Making his way to my desk was a tall, dark-haired boy with piercing green eyes. He was attractive, to say the least. He wore the school uniform in a way which made it look cool. When his gaze finally meets mine a wave of shock and utter surprise flashes across his face. But he quickly covers it up, replacing it with a glare. His pace slows as he reaches my desk, or should I say his desk? Assuming he is Chase Rivers.

I'm unsure of what to do as he stands there and narrows his eyes at me. Should I move? Should I see what happens? Maybe he'll let me have his seat? Judging by the look on his perfectly sculpted face I am guessing that

that is not the case. I don't need to look around the classroom to notice that everyone is watching. Great, I won't even survive first period.

After what feels like forever he finally clears his throat, "You're in my seat." I gulp.

Suddenly, as if the heavens have opened up, a commanding voice sounds from the front of the classroom, "Mr Rivers is there a reason as to why you're holding up my class? If not then please take a seat."

Chase is still looking at me. I feel like I'm a specimen being examined by a scientist. He then turns around and scans the room for a seat. The only spare seat is one in the second row. He shifts his gaze back to me and then slowly saunters over and sits down.

I notice everyone's eye on me. "Ah yes, we have a new student. Welcome to my literature class Sage Hill," Mr Red says before turning his back towards the board and writing today's lesson plan. I don't need a mirror to know my face is now a shade of crimson red.

I try to pay attention but my gaze keeps drifting over to the back of Chase River's head. Have I just made myself an enemy? A very attractive enemy. I can't stop replaying what had just happened over and over again in my mind. So much for blending in.

What a fabulous start! Not.

Chapter 4 ~ Chase

Chase's POV

The interrogation room at the police station is small and square, different from sitting in the principal's office talking to the police. That place is comfortable and familiar, I had been there numerous times before. This room is different however, uncomfortable and cold. There is no clock to keep track of how long I have been here, it is unnerving.

Sitting on one side of the heavy steel table, I assess the man in front of me on the other side. His face is stern yet friendly, around his eyes are laughter lines, he is tanned and quite tall. Rubbing his hands tiredly over his face he stares up at me, as if he is fed up and waiting for me to tell him something he doesn't already know.

The disappointing thing for him is that I don't have anything new to tell him that I didn't tell the police a week ago in the principal's office. Nothing has changed. He wasn't the only one wishing Brett would just show up with his signature smirk and cocky attitude.

Putting his notes on the table, glaring at me in an uncomfortable silence I look up to meet his gaze. With determination and intimidation, I am refusing to break eye contact or be the first to speak.

"Hi Mr Rivers, I'm inspector Mark Hill, I'm just here to go over the information you've told the police about the disappearance of Brett Reed"

I nod my head as I glance at the papers on the table and then fixate my gaze back on his face, expressionless. Hill, where do I know that name from? Oh shit, that's the new girl's surname, I wonder whether she's his daughter? Her father's the new Inspector, figures, probably where she gets her courage from, sitting in my spot.

"So according to these notes you know Brett Reed quite well and people could even go as far as to call you friends. When suddenly a bit over a week ago, a few hours before Brett goes missing you and Brett have a physical fight in the parking lot?"

Fidgeting restlessly in my seat uncomfortably, I nod. Clearing my throat, I snap back with a quick "yes" before he goes on.

"Yes, what. You were friends, you had a fight?" his eyes are squinting at me questionably, inviting me to continue.

"We used to be friends when we were younger, our families were friends, but people change, circumstances change and I haven't known that Brett for a while".

Raising his eyebrows, he continues, "No one knew why the two of you suddenly started fighting but people say that they saw the two of you having a heated discussion before the brawl broke out, what was that about?"

Looking up and meeting his gaze square on I don't answer, so he continues.

"And that was the last time Brett Reed was seen, having a fight with you, so you can't blame everyone for wondering what happened between you two that made him suddenly disappear"

"How would I know where he is, I don't keep tabs on him," I say growing more aggravated by the minute.

"I don't know or care where he's gone or why he's gone. I left. I walked off and went home. I was just as surprised as you were that he was gone the next day," I snap fed up.

"Are we done here, can I leave?" I say standing with such force that my chair falls over behind me.

"For now, but I'll be in touch, Mr Rivers",

Storming out the door, I turn the corner trying to escape the questioning eyes of those around me.

As I rush around the corner without realising how quick I'm going I crash into someone, sending them flying to the ground with a thud.

"Owwww, watch where you're going!" the person cries out. as papers go flying everywhere.

I look down and my eyes widen with surprise, out of all the possible people to run into it had to be her. Great now the detective will have me for assault and battery on his daughter. Was the universe against me?

"What the hell, watch where you're going! What are you stalking me now?" I growl.

She looks up and her eyes widen with recognition but instead of the fear that I'm accustomed to receiving, the only emotion present in her eyes is annoyance. That as well as embarrassment as her cheeks turn a crimson red. "Am I stalking you? You're the one that ran into me," she states aggravated.

Trying to hide my faltering smile, I scan her up and down, taking in her appearance with her auburn coloured hair that cascades down to below her shoulders framing her small round face. She has pale skin and bright observing eyes that are sharp and alert.

My frown deepens, how did I manage to run into the same girl twice in one day, when I'm doing my best to avoid everyone or their doing their best to avoid me since Brett's disappearing act.

"And by the way, you don't own that seat that I was sitting in this morning, it's school property," she blurts out.

I glare down at her and a scowl crosses onto my face. I push past her and keep walking towards the exit.

"Bye then," I hear her mutter under her breath. Is she for real?

Stalking towards the door I push it open with such force the glass rattles.

I leave without a second glance.

Chapter 5 ~ Sage

I watch as Chase stalks past me and heads towards the door. He doesn't even look back at me as he walks through the glass doors. I mean, why would he? He probably thinks I'm such a creep. First I take his seat and then I crash into him at the police station.

And I thought today couldn't get any worse! Well, I suppose it wasn't too bad. Alice was nice and introduced me to two of her other friends who seemed equally as sweet. In fact, my first day at my new school was quite alright if you excluded my two encounters with Chase Rivers. Oh, and also being referred to as 'The girl who sat in Chase River's seat,' in the hallways. I mean seriously, what is this school? It's just a seat!

Suddenly, a young police officer walks out of a nearby office and gives me an odd look. Only then do I realise how strange I look. I'm still sitting on the cold, tiled floor of the town's police station. I've dropped my bag containing a file my father left at home and asked me to quickly rush in. I give the officer a sheepish grin and quickly hurry to pick up the bag I dropped when I crashed into Chase Rivers. Or Chase Rivers crashed into me. Whichever really.

As I walk down the hallway in search of my father's office I begin to wonder why Chase was at the police station to begin with. Maybe someone stole something from him? Like maybe a dog, or his car or... his seat. I push that thought out of my head, knowing how stupid it would be for him to report me for stealing his spot. Imagine going to jail for sitting in Chase Rivers' literature seat. I chuckle to myself, earning another weird look from a passing by police officer.

I find my father's office, tucked away in the corner of the police station and tap my knuckles against the door. As I wait for the door to open I look around. Across from my father's office is what looks to be the interrogation room and next to that is another office. I hear a creak as he gets up from his chair and hear his footsteps make their way over to the door. It swings open.

My father stands there, his dark hair a bit of a mess and his blue eyes looking tired. I have my mother's auburn hair and my father's clear blue eyes.

"Thanks, Sage! I can't believe I left it at home," he says as I hand him the file.

"No worries," I smile.

"So how was your first day at school?" He asks as he walks back into his office and sits down at his desk. I follow him in.

"It was alright. I made three friends. How was work?" I ask, eager to divert the topic of conversation.

I look around the office. It's an uncomfortable space, very cold and quiet. The only sign of life is my father's desk which is covered with papers, photos and documents. I notice a photo of whom I predict to be Brett Reed in the corner. He is tan with blonde hair and wears a smug grin in the picture.

"Not too bad, just been working on the case. Talking to people, finding out information and going over details," he nods, rubbing his eyes as if it will help him to stay awake.

At that moment a police officer pokes his head through the door. It's the same one who heard me laugh to myself in the hallway. Great. He thankfully chooses to ignore my presence and looks over to my father.

"Detective Hill, we need you to come look at something quickly," he asks, obviously not being specific because I'm in the room.

"Ah, yes, of course, Dylan," my dad says, getting up from his desk and putting the file I just gave him into his desk drawer. "I'll see you at home Sage," he says looking at me. I give him a nod and a smile before exiting the office, avoiding eye contact with the officer.

I walk down the hallway, trying to remember my way out of the building. I become very aware of my father and the officer Dylan walking a fair distance behind me, talking in hushed tones. I wonder if they're talking about Chase?

Desperate to know if he's the topic of their conversation, I quickly bend down, pretending to tie my already tied shoelace. I strain my ears and my pulse quickens.

"Did the Rivers kid give any new information?" Officer Dylan asks, clear distaste rolling off his tongue as he mentions Chase's surname.

"Nope, only information that we already know," I hear my father sigh.

I thought my father was solely working on Brett Reed's disappearance case. Why was he interviewing Chase Rivers? Maybe another officer was away and he had to quickly fill in. But wouldn't they get a different officer like Dylan to do that rather than a detective?

"Don't worry. I assume he'll open up soon. There's only so much kids can keep to themselves before it eats away at them," Officer Dylan says. What does Chase need to open up about? Their footsteps come to a stop and I realise they must be standing outside a door.

"So what did we need to talk about?" My father asks.

I realise how long I've been 'tying my shoe laces up for' and slowly stand up. As I begin to slowly walk down the office towards the door I only just make out Officer Dylan's next words.

"Whether Brett Reed is, in fact, alive or presumed dead," he sighs. And with that I quickly hurry through the doors of the station before I can hear my father's response.

Dead. As in non-living. Someone in Mapleville, my age could be dead. Murdered. A chill runs down my spine as I glance around at the quiet street I am now walking down. I am living in a town with a murderer.

I curse myself as I remember that Officer Dylan did not state he was dead, but could be. The last thing I should be doing is rushing to conclusions. If I was any real danger my dad would not be letting me walk these streets alone, let alone living in a town with a murderer on the loose.

Brett has been missing for over a week now, leaving no evidence to his whereabouts behind. No wonder the police are thinking the worst.

Many questions start floating around my head as I push the topic of Brett Reed to the side. Will the desirably good looking Chase Rivers kill me for crashing into him? Should I drop out of literature in fear of another encounter? Why was Chase at the police station? Why did my father interview him if he's only working on the Brett Reed case?

As I nearly walk into a park bench it suddenly occurs to me. My father's words slowly play over in my head, "Talking to people, finding out information and going over details." Chase must have something to do with the case. That's why my father was interviewing him. Maybe he knows something. But then why were the officer and my father talking about him not opening up?

I sigh, confused with my own questions that are floating around my head, pestering to be answered.

~~~~~~~~~~~~~~~~~~~~

☆ Please vote ☆

Leave a comment letting me know your thoughts on the story so far
~~~~~~~~~~~~~~~~~~~~

Chapter 6 ~ Chase

C hase's POV

Throughout my room, the alarm is blaring and unceasing. I look over at the clock that reads 7.43. With a grunt, I scan my room and heave the covers off me. I get in the shower and get ready. As I storm downstairs my mother's voice calls out from the kitchen.

"Would you like any breakfast?" she calls after me, hoping my response is going to be different from every other morning.

"Nope," I tell her as I grab and an apple, kiss her on the cheek and leave without a second glance.

I jump in my car and speed off to school, thinking about the day before me. I wasn't in the mood to talk to anyone. I sure as hell couldn't be bothered to walk through the corridors again and have everyone's eyes on me watching, and whispering behind me, as I go through the day. I liked lurking in the shadows assessing others, observing and calculating. It was hard when everyone's eyes were on me. I was usually the one that everyone tried to not think about.

Scanning the car park for my usual spot I notice a white car parked in my spot, my brows crinkle in confusion. You've got to be kidding me. Everyone knows this is my car parking spot, it might as well have a bright red sign saying Chase Rivers on it. To say I am annoyed is an understatement. Is someone really wanting to challenge me, if so they have chosen the wrong day to do it. I would have thought they would be afraid that I might make them go missing along with Brett, considering everyone already thinks that I have something to do with it.

Immediately catching my attention is who steps out of the car. I should have known. Of course, this little auburn red head would have the nerve to park in my spot. Is this girl obsessed with me or is she just plain clueless? My anger increased as I sped off in search of a new spot tightening my hold on the wheel making my knuckles go white. I considered nudging her car with mine, after all, mine was a wreck there would be no damage to my car but hers, and with her father being the detective and all, I don't think she the right person to be picking a battle with. I find one far away from my usual spot, in front of the doors and as if the universe hates me, I hear the bell ring. Great. I am late. I wouldn't be surprised if the detective questions me on this as well considering how close he has been watching me recently. At least I can say it is his daughter's fault for parking in my spot.

Stalking into school and looking around the empty corridors I let out a grunt of annoyance. Biology is the class I am meant to be in right now. I walk in noticing how almost all sets of eyes in the classroom snap to me, including the teacher. What was going on, no one ever really cared if I existed and now I'm the centre of everyone's attention.

"Mr Rivers, late again I see. Care to explain why?"

"Well you see I was told to go to hell and on my quest to find it I got side tract. But no worries because I've finally found it," I reply not caring to give her a second glance as I saunter down an isle and dump my books onto the table with a loud thud. I ignore the shocked looks of my classmates as I sit down and look at the clock, noting that I shouldn't have even bothered to come to this class considering how long was left.

My eyes scan the class and I notice the reason for me being late is sitting right next to me, drawing away in her notebook trying to not pay attention to what was happening around her or even bothering to look up at me, unlike with the rest of the class. I smirk, unlucky for her, if there is one class that you should pay attention to or at least look like you're concentrating, it is this one.

"Ms Hill, would you like to tell us the answer to the next question?"

My smirk widens as I watch her head snap up at the sound of her name. Sage squirms in her seat as her cheeks turn red in embarrassment. It is quite pleasing to watch. Not many things brought me enjoyment these days but this was one of them as I turned to stare directly at her.

"Errrrrrr yea its ummm..." the sound of the bell rings through the classroom, making Sage sigh in relief. Damn, I was actually enjoying watching the good girl scramble, I think as I smile to myself.

I stalk out of the classroom and go to my locker just as an announcement rings over the speakers, catching the attention of everyone in the corridor.

"Can all students please report to the assembly hall immediately," the principle's stern voice announces filling the corridor.

I let out an annoyed sigh and head in the direction of the hall with a frown on my face. Walking in I realise I'm one of the last students to enter. My eyes meet with the familiar ones of the detective and the principle, I give them a smirk as I sit in my seat, making the principal frown back at me, his dislike for my attitude apparent.

The quiet whispers that are filling the hall are hushed as the principle speaks up.

"As you all know, Brett Reed is a student who has been attending this school up until a few weeks ago is missing," his gaze scans the room stopping at me and I raise my eyebrows and roll my eyes in annoyance.

The whispers start up again as some people glance up at me to see if I have any reaction. Too bad for them I keep my face blank as I stare ahead. Some people just need to mind their own god damn business.

"Silence please, as I was saying, there has been no new information on his whereabouts and we now have to assume the worst". You could hear a pin drop with how silent it was.

I could feel one pair of crystal blue eyes stand out among the rest, they were wide with fear and curiosity as she turns and glances straight at me. Our eyes lock making her look away almost instantly. She must have heard the rumours, the talk of other students. The unspoken new rule of Maple High. To steer clear of Chase Rivers at all costs.

Just one look told me everything I needed to know. I know what she's thinking. The same thing almost everyone in the room is probably thinking.

Everyone's minds and opinions on what happened were already made up. Not that I was bothered. I couldn't care less what they thought. These people meant nothing to me. They never had, and nothing was going to change now.

I waited behind as everyone left the hall, followed by the principal and Detective Hill.

"Mr Rivers," the detective says with a curt nod of the head.

"Mark," I say with a cocky smirk.

"It's Mr Hill for you," he corrects me not looking pleased with my response.

"No worries, Mark," I say as I flash a cheeky grin, satisfied that I could get under his skin so easily.

And with a smirk, I get up out of the seat and walk out of the hall.

Chapter 7 ~ Sage

S AGE'S POV

"And we now have to assume the worst."

I hear a few gasps and chokes from around the room. The words send a shiver down my spine. I notice people glance at a certain someone sitting near the back. I follow their gaze to an expressionless Chase Rivers. His dark hair is messy as if he just woke up. My pulse quickens as his green eyes meet mine. I quickly look away, my cheeks burning.

Students begin to stand up, making a beeline for the door. I steal one glance at Chase over my shoulder and see he's yet to have moved. I follow the rest of the students out of the assembly hall, eavesdropping into multiple conversations at once.

"I can't believe it! He's gone?"

"Brett Reed can't be dead, he's Brett Reed!"

"I think I'm going to cry!"

"I don't understand! Why Brett?"

I tune into the discussion May, Alice and Sarah are having about the horrifying news we've just been told.

"Oh! Your poor Dad Sage! This must be so stressful!" May sighs, giving me a sympathetic look. "I thought this kind of stuff only happened in movies!"

"Why Mapleville of all places?" Alice ponders out loud as we come to a stop near our lockers.

I look around at the many students huddled together in the hallway. Most look terrified, some even crying. Others seem excited at the idea that a murder case could be happening in their town. I don't even need to have known Brett Reed to know the impact he has had on these people's lives. I guess he was their star, their idea of perfection in such a small, isolated town.

"So do you guys believe the rumours? Do you really think Chase Rivers is capable of murder?" Sarah asks as she tugs nervously on her brown hair.

"Why do people believe he has something to do with it?" I ask intrigued.

"He and Brett have a weird history," Alice says. "They used to be best friends, inseparable in fact. Both good football players. Brett was the boy with good grades who the teachers all loved while Chase was always more on the naughty side. They were the 'It' duo. But then something happened," she trails off, lost in thought.

"What do you mean 'something happened,'" I ask in confusion. Friends break apart all the time. What did that have to do with a possible murder?

"Nobody knows. One day they were best mates and the next day they wouldn't dare go near each other. Chase dropped out of the football team and stopped making the effort to interact with others. Brett became more guarded. That was a year ago," May sighs.

"Some people think it's because Brett was worried Chase would take over as captain of the football team, while others say that Brett didn't want to find himself too deep into Chase's troubles," Sarah says.

"But that's not all," Alice adds. "The day before Brett disappeared they had a fight in the parking lot. Well, a heated conversation that escalated into a bit of a brawl. They hadn't talked to each other in a year and then BOOM! It was during the fifth period, one class saw it happen from their window."

My mind races with thoughts.

"What I would give to know why they stopped being friends," Sarah sighs, leaning against her locker.

"Why didn't anyone ask?" I enquire.

"Oh, people tried. A guy called Max asked Chase and was met with a fist that broke his nose," Sarah says sympathetically.

"And you can't forget about Rachel! She was dating Brett at the time. She decided to ask him what happened and right then and there in the cafeteria he dumped her in front of everyone," Alice says. "She didn't return to school for a week because she was so embarrassed."

We make our way to the cafeteria for lunch. Classes have been cancelled until the afternoon so we could fully process the information about Brett Reed's possible murder. Looking around at the other students in the cafeteria I come to the conclusion that they're definitely going to need more than a few hours to recover. We sit down at a table in the corner.

"I don't believe he's dead!" May exclaims suddenly. "He can't be! He's Brett Reed! Mapleville without Brett is like a sandwich without butter! It's nothing without it!"

"Calm down May, his death isn't even confirmed," Alice says.

"Aww does May still have a crush on Brett from 9th grade?" Sarah asks teasingly, smiling at a bright red May.

"I do not! Why would I bother wasting my time crushing on a guy who doesn't even know I exist," she sighs, her hazel eyes filled with longing. "Let alone if he even exists anymore."

Right at that moment, a hush falls over the cafeteria as many conversations come to a halt. There in the doorway stands the mysterious Chase Rivers. Aware everyone's attention is on him, he scans the cafeteria with a glare as if to say 'mind your own business.' It works as everyone quickly turns away.

I keep my eyes trained on him as he skips the lunch line, grabbing himself some food. Nobody in the queue even questions his lack of patience, simply averting their glances. He saunters over to the door.

Before exiting, he slowly turns around. His eyes scan the room and then suddenly land on me. I feel my heart skip a beat. He narrows his green eyes. Then Chase Rivers does the last thing I would have expected of him. His glare turns into an amused grin as he sends a quick wink my way. I feel my cheeks go bright red and quickly try to hide my face so he can't see my reaction, but he's already gone.

I look back at my new friends who are all looking at me with wide eyes.

"Did I just imagine it or did Chase Rivers just wink at you?" Sarah asks shocked.

"Nope! I saw it too! And he smiled! He actually smiled at you, Sage!" May squeals with a large smile on her face. "Maybe he likes you!

Chase Rivers? Liking me? I highly doubt it! Not after I stole his seat and ran into him at the police station. Besides, a wink and a grin doesn't mean he likes me, it means he's cocky and arrogant.

"You're forgetting the fact that he may have had something to do with the Brett Reed case. He doesn't exactly scream safety," Alice says, giving May a warning look.

"He probably only winked because he had something in his eye," I say, convincing myself that that was it.

Yet I can't ignore that weird feeling I got when I saw the forever frowning Chase Rivers smiling at me.

Chapter 8 ~ Chase

Chase's POV

The sound of the door opening echoes throughout the cafeteria. All the noise that could be heard from the outside, the chatter of students trying to talk over one another to be heard is silenced as I stroll into the room. I let my eyes wander the cafeteria and glare at people who have the courage to stare at me. I hate the cafeteria. Hate the curious eyes. The constant gossip. It isn't me. Never has been.

The only time I had sat in here was when Brett had pushed me about it. He said he had to keep up his reputation. No one knew the truth. It was pathetic really, he was just as bad as his parents were when it came to image. I of all people knew how easy it was for your reputation to be ruined by the click of a finger.

I stroll to the front of the queue, watching amusedly as everyone just unconsciously moves out of my way. Are they all actually this afraid of me, the thought makes me smirk. I turn and make my way to the exit not wanting to be in here any longer than needed.

I can feel their prying eyes follow me, as I turn, I meet a pair of azure blue eyes that belong to Sage, they were wide and curious filled with unanswered questions. Well if everyone wants a show, I'll give them a show. I do the thing that no one would expect me to do. I send Sage a wink and wait patiently with raised eyebrows and a smirk as blood pools her cheeks making her cast her gaze downwards as if she suddenly found the table in front of her very interesting. As everyone's eyes divert from me to where I am looking, I know the controversy and drama that wink will cause, but honestly, I couldn't care less. If I'm going down I may as well bring the detectives daughter down with me. Watching Sage squirm was just way too amusing. With a chuckle I walk out, waiting for the gossip to start about that one action.

Not long after lunch, I head towards my car ready to go home. Classes are cancelled until this afternoon due to the meeting in the gym. But I sure as hell am not going to stick around to wait for them to recommence.

Getting home I jump out of the car and stride up the steps in one bound opening the front door I look around the hallway, filled with old family photos of a happier time, suddenly coming home wasn't such a good idea. One glance at those photos and I want to throw up. They were a reminder of older, happier times when things were easy and secrets were unknown.

"Chase, honey is that you?" Mum's soft voice calls from the kitchen.

"Yep," I say as I enter the kitchen and head towards the fridge.

"Why are you home so early, doesn't school finish in a couple of hours?"

"Yeah, it was cancelled," I say my tone sharp as I shut the fridge with a bang, cutting the conversation short.

"Ok," she says. Only then do I realise how tired she actually looks, the dark circles under her green eyes are prominent. I frown down at her.

"How late were you up last night?" I ask.

Glancing sheepishly at me from under her dark eyelashes, I already know the answer.

"Not too late, I was just looking through the jobs currently being advertised. We need the money, it's been a bit tight, you know since he left," she trails off, her words becoming quieter as she speaks.

Asshole, I don't care that he left us, I got over it, but mum will never be the same, her perfect world shattered and crumpled at her feet.

By the look on her face, I could tell there was a burning curiosity hidden behind her tired eyes to ask about Brett. One glance silences her question before it even leaves her tongue. I was not ready to speak to anybody about this. And I don't know if I ever will.

"I'll be back soon, don't wait up for me," I tell her as I kiss her cheek and stroll out of the house grabbing my keys off the hook as I go.

I probably should think through the rash decisions I make but I'm Maplesville's delinquent, outcast and now apparent murderer so why should I give a damn about anything or anyone. With that thought in mind, I race to the place I swore I'd never come back to. The place that 3 years ago mum and Brett both begged me not to go to and I listened. I stayed away. But not anymore. This needs to be done. We need the money and I need a release of this built up anger and frustration.

Glancing up at the old worn warehouse, the paint peeling off the walls with the dents and graffiti engraved on it, I knew I was back to where I had once belonged. I walk around to the back door, that at first glance you wouldn't think existed. Scanning the card that I had told mum I threw out, I waited for the familiar click, unlocking the security door.

Pushing it open I embrace the smell of blood and sweat as I hear grunts of pain and the smashing of leather gloves connecting with flesh. I knew that sound all too well, however, it was a rare occasion that I was the one who left the ring batted and bruised.

As a man approaches me, I assess him with hard eyes as I don't recognise him. He looks like he almost belongs, but not quite, he doesn't have the look of a fighter, more a scammer. His eyes are hidden by a pair of shades, he lifts them as he speaks to me.

"Looking to place a bet here son?" he asks me.

"No, came to see Aaron," I tell him my tone hard and cold, I learnt long ago to never show weakness in a place like this.

"Aaron aye? And what's a kid like you needing to see the boss about?"

"Don't see how that's your business, now is he in the office or not?" I demand and watch as his confident façade crumbles a bit. Weak scum, I think to myself, probably never fought a fight in his life.

"Errrrr.. right down that hall to the right," he states as he scurries off in the direction he came from.

Following his directions, I see the large wooden door with a golden label on it, "Aaron". Only he would ensure he got a name tag in the colour of victory. I fist the door and without waiting for a reply, push it open and saunter into the room. I watch as he looks up, his gaze angry and hard, ready to scold whoever has had the nerve to walk into his office without permission. Watching as his eyes flash with recognition as he settles into the back of his chair, his gaze on me. I smirk in reply.

"Well I don't believe my eyes, is Chase Rivers really back, what do I owe the pleasure?"

"I need you to set me up with some fights, and lots of them."

"Now, now, Chase, slow down. You've been out of the game for a while, what makes you think you're up for it and what's more, what's in it for me?" he hasn't changed a bit. Still looking for any way to make himself some cash. But I knew not to fall for his tricks.

"You'll have what you always wanted, me to fight for you and this time it'll be on your side, representing you," I knew he wouldn't turn this down. He had always wanted this, he tried persuading me 3 years ago when I was unbeaten, constantly beating his fighters.

"And with that Chase you have yourself a deal," he holds out his hand an unusual smile graces his face.

I nod my head and slide my hand into his and with a firm shake, I know there's no going back.

I've made a deal with the devil himself.

~~~~~~~~~~~~~~~~~~~~

☆ Please vote ☆
~~~~~~~~~~~~~~~~~~~~

Chapter 9 ~ Sage

S AGE'S POV

I groan as my persistent alarm clock goes off for the third time this morning. I finally will myself to open my eyes but immediately regret doing so as soon as I see the bright light flooding through my windows. How I hate Mondays!

I slowly get up and make my way to my bathroom. The perks of being an only child. I shudder as the cold water from the tap makes contact with my face. Why can't the weekend be three days instead of two? Feeling too lazy to do anything special with my hair, I decide to just go with a messy bun.

I quickly put my uniform on and head towards the kitchen. There sits my father at the table looking like the definition of tired. As I get closer I can clearly make out the exhaustion present on his face. The case is clearly taking a toll on him. I don't think he has ever dealt with such a bizarre mystery before. Usually, when someone goes missing there's normally a few little clues left over but it's as if Brett Reed has disappeared off the face of the Earth entirely. Maybe Aliens do exist.

He looks up as I approach, giving me a strained smile. "Good morning."

"Morning Dad," I say, leaning down and giving him a kiss on the forehead. "What's on the agenda today?"

"Well I'll be coming to school today," he says.

"Again?" I ask, referring to the past Friday, the last thing I want is my dad constantly being at my school. It's bad enough being the new kid as it is.

"Yes, we are going to interview some more students. Try and get some more information on who Brett really was. I mean is," he says sighing.

I nod and turn on the television to catch the morning news. The screen immediately flashes to a middle-aged woman and man. The lady has blonde hair and looks very distressed. The man, on the other hand, seems angry.

"Brett's parents," my dad says. I quickly grab the remote and turn the volume up.

"We just want him home," Mrs Reed pleas. "If anyone has any information, don't hold back. Say something before it's too late," and with that she bursts into tears, turning away from the camera recording her.

"Whoever took Brett will pay," the man concludes before dragging his wife away.

I turn to look at my father whose attention is captivated by the TV.

"Do they know anything about who might have something to do with it?" I ask.

"Mr Reed put forward one name," he responds, running a hand through his hair.

"Chase Rivers?" I ask, trying to hide my interest.

My dad immediately looks at me, "How do you know that?" He demands.

"Oh, I just figured because he was at the police station the day I went in to give you the file you forgot," I say nonchalantly.

He nods and sits down again, "How do you know him?"

"School," I say.

I look at the time and almost faint. School starts in 13 minutes. I guess I'm taking the car again. I quickly grab a banana and my school bag and head for the door. I call out a quick goodbye to my dad and get in the car.

I spend the drive to school pondering how I could help my dad out with the case. I mean surely there is something I could do. He always seems worried and stressed lately.

I look around the school parking lot for a park. I notice the place where I parked in on Friday is vacant and quickly make my way towards it.

Just as I'm getting ready to turn into it, a car coming from the opposite direction takes it. I let out a frustrated sigh. It was clearly mine first. I watch as the thief hops out of his car and nearly choke when I see who it is. The annoyingly handsome Chase. He turns towards me, a smirk plastered on his face. I roll my eyes at him and continue driving.

For someone who is a suspect in a potential murder case, he seems quite calm.

I finally walk through the school doors with two minutes to spare. I make a beeline for my locker where May is waiting for me.

"Look who finally decided to show up!" She smiles.

"I would have been here much earlier if a certain someone who goes by the name Chase Rivers didn't steal my car spot. I had to park so far away!" I whine, grabbing my books from my locker.

"Well, I guess that makes it even. You stole his seat, he stole your car spot," she laughs.

The bell rings and we quickly say goodbye. I walk down the hallway past the scrambling students who don't want to be late for class.

I enter my biology class and take a seat at the front. No way was I ever going near the back of any classroom ever again!

Our teacher Ms Oliver enters the classroom. In her hands are multiples papers and she begins to go around the classroom distributing them. Oh crap! Since when did we have a test? I knew I should have been paying more attention in class!

My stress is put to ease when I realise the paper that has just been planted on my desk is in fact not a test but a sheet that reads 'Assignment.'

"As you can see you will all be doing an assignm-" Ms Oliver comes to a stop as Chase waltzes through the door as if he has all the time in the world. She gives him a stern look and waits until he takes a seat (which is of course at the back) before continuing. "As I was saying, you will be doing an assignment on Osmosis. You will be doing it in pairs and will have four lessons to do it. If you are unable to finish it in these lessons then you will have to do it in your own time. Any questions?" She asks.

"Can we choose our partners?" A guy who I believe is called Harry asks. No, no, no! The one class in which I don't have a friend.

"Yes you can, but if I see anyone misusing their time then some adjustments will be made," Ms Oliver says looking around the classroom.

Why couldn't she just choose our partners for us? Actually, why can't I just do the project on my own? Maybe if everyone chooses their partner I'll be the only one left over. Fingers crossed.

I look around the classroom and have to do a double take when I notice everyone has already chosen their partner. Well almost everyone. My eyes land on Chase Rivers who gives me his classic smirk.

Why did the universe hate me so much? What did I do wrong? I quickly look around the classroom again and notice everyone sitting with a partner. I see Ms Oliver give me a sympathetic look.

Suddenly an idea hits me so fast that I nearly fall off my chair. This is how I could help my dad! I could get to know Chase and find out if he has anything to do with Brett's disappearance. If he does have something to do with it then I can find out what that is but if he doesn't then I can tell my dad he's looking in the wrong direction.

Suddenly, my brilliant plan is interrupted, "Looks like you're stuck with me," someone grunts.

I squeal, nearly jumping out of my skin. I hear a deep laugh as I look up and see Chase towering over me. I roll my eyes at him and muster the best death glare I can manage. However, to my dismay, it doesn't even faze him.

Chase's dark hair looks the same as it does most days, as if he just woke up. Planted on his face is his signature smirk, mirroring the one he gave me this morning when he stole my car spot.

"Why so glum?" He asks with a grin that makes my pulse quicken as his green eyes focus on mine. "Don't you want to be my partner?" He asks sarcastically, feigning hurt.

"No, not particularly," I say sweetly.

He lets out a loud laugh, gaining the attention of a few people near us who give us a mixed variety of looks. Some look sympathetic, some jealous even. Most just seem surprised to be hearing a laugh come out of Chase's mouth.

He drags a chair from another table over. "So what do you know about Osmosis?" I ask, eager to get into the project.

"Never heard of it," he says grabbing one of my pencils, and flicking it around in his hands.

"My name's Sage," I say, taking the pencil out of his hands.

"Oh, so we are doing formal introductions? Well I doubt I need to introduce myself to you, you've probably already heard all about me from the lifeless gossipers in this town," he says in a bored tone.

Not knowing what to say to that I grab my pencil out of his hand and start writing.

~~~~~~~~~~~~~~~~~~~~~~~

☆ Please vote and leave a comment ☆
~~~~~~~~~~~~~~~~~~~~~~~

Chapter 10 ~ Chase

C hase's POV

    I sit back, assess and watch, as my thoughts get drowned out by the sounds of people gathering and scrambling to pick their best friends as their partners. Wow, how pathetic, I mean it is only a project. Some look around pleased and relieved with who they end up with, while others sit with frowns and looks of disappointment, glancing at who they had wanted to be paired with and look distastefully at their partners.

I'm happy to work on my own because then I can float through and not have someone obsess over what I'm doing or if I've completed my section. I mean what did they expect? That I was going to do it? They should have known. Every time they would get their hopes up, thinking that I was going to change my ways for them then I would crush them when I walked in empty handed with a careless attitude. Most get mad and ask the teacher why and how they got stuck with me. I don't care. Never did. Never had.

My hopes of everyone finding their own partners and getting to work alone were short lived when my gaze lands on a certain girl with her head turned towards the window, either deep in thought or like me trying to work alone. I had heard she was smart, so she would probably prefer to work alone than be dragged down by someone who doesn't know what they're doing. I can't help but notice that people begin to watch as I stroll up to Sage's seat. She's the only person who isn't paying attention to my every move.

"Looks like your stuck with me," I say and watch as she sucks in a deep breath and her cheeks blush with embarrassment as she jumps in fright and glares at me. I chuckle to myself and watch as her eyes scan the classroom to see who's watching us but by now everyone is too busy discussing their plans for the project to spare us a second glance.

I watch as she musters up her best attempt at a glare, too bad for her she looks nothing close to intimidating. But I decided to humour her.

"Why so glum?" I say with a grin.

"Don't you want to be my partner?" I say pretending to actually care what she thinks.

To my surprise she looks up at me with a new flame of determination in her eyes, "No, not particularly."

I slide into a nearby seat unable to stop the laugh that rumbles out of my chest.

"So what do you know about osmosis?" she asks. I grab her pencil and start flicking it around.

"Never heard of it," I say tuning out.

"My name's Sage," she says with determination as she tries to steal her pencil out of my hand.

"Oh, so we are doing formal introductions? Well I doubt I need to introduce myself to you, you've probably already heard all about me from the lifeless gossipers in this town," I say unable to hide the bite to my tone. I watch as her cheeks flush as she looks down regathering her thoughts and starts to write.

She glances at the clock and turns back to me. Is she dying to get rid of me that quickly?

"Since the bell is about to go are you free after school to plan and catch up on what we want to do?"

Maybe she doesn't want to get rid of me, she'd be the only person wanting to spend any time with Chase Rivers, at the moment, with everything going on.

My mind wanders back to the phone call I received earlier.

"No," I tell her bluntly. Hoping that she isn't deterred and might ask another time.

"Why?" she pries curiously. "What have you got to do that's so important?"

"None of your business," I tell her, watching as the curiosity is killed with disappointment. Good. Answers lead to more questions and I was not in the mood to sit here and play buddies with Sage just yet.

I get up and make my way towards the door.

"Chase come back and continue working the bell hasn't gone yet" the teacher's scolding voice bellows as I walk towards the door. I turn back and smirk at her as I wait. The sound of the bell ringing makes the teacher give me a pointed look and a huff as she turns her back to me. My smirk widens as I stroll out of the door towards the parking lot.

School's over and I need to be prepared for my fight that's lined up for tonight and every other night this week. Aaron was testing my limits. Trying to see whether I would stick it out and be a good investment of his time. I make my way towards the gym, jump out of the car and make my way towards the building.

I embrace the smell of sweat and dried blood. It has already started to become familiar again. My eyes lock onto a pair of harsh grey ones, that's warm hue disappeared a long time ago. His mouth raises into a smile that has no warmth in it, and he places his drink on a nearby table as he pushes past people making his way towards where I'm standing.

"Chase," he says acknowledging me.

"Aaron" I nod my head in his direction.

"I'm expecting a good fight tonight, no funny business, no playing," I nod as if I'm actually listening to what he's telling me. My mind is already in the ring pre-empting every move of tonight's fight. Playing out the different possibilities.

The siren for the fight to begin roars and rocks the cheap walls of the gym. This is a sound I am familiar with.

Stepping into the ring, I assess the person in front of me. He's big and his eyes are hungry and unforgiving, ready for the kill. The smell of alcohol flows off him in waves. His stance is eager and unbalanced. He's sloppy and messy, just by his posture I can tell he has no technique. If there was one thing that was drilled into me since I was young, it was that no matter what's happening, keep a stoic face and never show any signs of a weakness.

The small crowd gather around and cheer, eager and ready for the fight to be underway. Some are busy still placing their bets trying to pick a winner at the last second. I zone out and focus. As the whistle sounds throughout the room, the jeering from the sides increases to a deafening pitch that makes my head begin to spin. The floor vibrates from the commotion and I lock eyes onto my opponent. His lips curl up into a snarl and I smirk in reply. Bring it on.

He advances towards me and forms a mediocre fist and sends it flying towards my face. I block it and send a punch to his stomach and then again to his cheek and watch as he falls to the floor grunting out in pain. Too easy.

The ump comes and yanks my hand up into the air announcing me the winner. Glancing at the crowd all I see is a bunch of grey meaningless faces, some elated with their bet and others disappointed. They weren't here for anything more than to place their bets and make a quick buck.

People chant my name and give me a pat on the back, as though we're friends like they know me, but to me, they are a means to an end. I stroll towards Aaron and watch as he gives me a wicked grin. He's pleased. Pleased that I won but most importantly pleased that I won for his reputation of training the best fighters.

"You were good out there tonight Chase, keep your phone on you, you'll hear from me about your upcoming fights."

I nod and hold my hand out waiting for the money. He slips his hand into his pocket and produces a crumpled envelope. I grasp it in my hands and nod in his direction. Before anything more can be said I turn and walk out without a second glance. I got what I came here for, money.

~~~~~~~~~~~~~~~~~~~~

☆ Please vote ☆
~~~~~~~~~~~~~~~~~~~~

Chapter 11 ~ Sage

S age's POV

Yesterday at school Alice informed me that we had a big dance coming up in a few weeks. Not wanting to leave things to the last minute, I decided that I'd wake up early this morning and go shopping for a dress.

The only problem is that Mapleville is a small town. If I were to buy a dress from one of the local shops I'd be sure to turn up on the night twinning with another girl unintentionally.

So here I am on a Saturday morning in the car driving to the closest shopping district which happens to be over four hours away.

Sarah, Alice and May offered to accompany me but having already chosen their dresses, I didn't want to bore them. 30 minutes into the journey and I'm already regretting that decision.

Thankfully, Dad let me borrow his car again or else it would have been a long trek on foot. I'm just praying I don't get lost.

~~~~~~~
~~~~~~~

When I finally pull up to the shops it's just past 11 am. Thank gosh, it isn't too busy yet. I'm planning to quickly find a dress and then quickly leave.

I make my way over to a small looking boutique on the corner. In its windows are formal looking dresses. One is a full-length baby blue colour and the other is a shorter pink dress. In the store is hundreds of more variations of the two dresses at the front but in different colours and neck styles.

After I come to the conclusion that nothing takes my fancy I move onto the next store. Once again, all very nice dresses but nothing that strikes me as 'the one.'

Moments like these make me miss my mother even more. I envy the girls who get to go on shopping trips with their mothers. I wish she were here right now. She had an eye for fashion and would have made this decision a lot easier and more enjoyable.

As I enter the third shop, I somehow know this will be the one. I walk slowly through the shop. There are dresses of every colour, style and pattern.

I scan the room and my eyes land on a beautiful red dress. It is full length and has a side slit. The top of the dress is embroiled with red flowers that add detail to the dress. It has a halter neck. I can't help but smile like an idiot as I look at it.

"Beautiful isn't it?" I quickly turn around and see the shop assistant smiling at me. "Very!" I exclaim.

"Do you want to try it on?" She asks.

"Oh yes please," I say getting excited.

She shows me to a fitting room. I quickly put the dress on, excited to see how it will look.

I gasp when I look in the mirror. It's definitely the one. I take my hair out of my ponytail. The red goes so well with my blue eyes and chestnut coloured hair. My mother would have loved it.

I end up buying it. Luckily it fitted my dads budget and left me quite enough money to go buy a smoothie from one of the cafes.

￼I sit down at one of the tables, exhausted from shopping. I take a sip of my mango smoothie and look around. The street is definitely a lot busier now. My phone buzzes and I look down to see a message from my dad.

Hey sweetie, I won't be home when you get back. There are some leftovers in the fridge. Don't wait up

I sigh and type back a quick ok:)

It then suddenly hits me that I don't have any shoes to wear. I look at the time on my phone,

1:37 pm. I get up and go in search of a shoe shop. It isn't a hard job considering there are multiple.

I go inside the first one, already knowing what I'm looking for. I want a pair of silver heels that will complement the rich red colour of the dress.

I scan the shoes and finally see a pair. I bring them to a lady working there and she goes out to the back of the store, in search of my size. I was unluckily blessed with big feet.

As I sit there waiting I look out the window. Two little kids walk by eating ice cream and walking in the other direction is a lady who seems to be barking orders into her phone. I'd hate to be on the other end of that phone call.

Across the road is a hooded figure who I think is a boy. He is dressed in black jeans and a black hoodie, quite extreme for a sunny day like today.

He walks quickly with his head down. He quickly looks around allowing me a glimpse of his face.

I almost choke. Actually, forget that. I almost die. Walking along the other side of the street is a guy who looks exactly like Brett Reed.

I tell myself I must be wrong. I'm tired from shopping after all! I must be a little delirious. But that tan skin, that blonde hair and that face just replicates the features of the boy who has been planted on missing posters all over Mapleville.

My legs stand up on their own will and drag me to the window. Curiosity sparks within me and I quickly grab my bags and leave the store.

As I walk out I hear the lady return, "I've found the shoes in your size.. wait! Where are you going?"

I ignore her and quicken my pace, desperate not to lose him. Shoes can wait!

I cross the road so I'm walking behind him. He keeps up a fast pace and I'm practically jogging to keep up. Crap! Maybe I should have stayed on the other side so he doesn't assume I'm following him. You wouldn't think I'm the daughter of a detective.

I don't know what part of me decides it'd be a good idea to call out his name, but regardless of that I do.

"Brett! Brett Reed!" I shout.

The hooded figure comes to an extreme halt. Then he keeps walking, faster this time. It's enough for me to know it must be him.

"Wait! Please," I shout as I run to meet his pace.

He doesn't. I quicken my pace to a sprint. Gosh, I should have never opened my mouth. He quickly turns around, causing me to nearly crash into him.

"Just leave me alone and don't tell anyone about this," he grunts. Brett looks stressed and tired. He quickly turns around again and continues walking, if you could call it that.

"Is it Chase? Is that why you're here?" I squeak out, praying his answer is a no and Chase will be in the clear. I don't know why I care, I'm just interested. At least that's what I'm telling myself.

He quickly turns around, "You're friends with Chase?" He asks, sounding interested.

I don't know what to say so I begin rambling instead, "Are we friends? Definitely not. I think he hates me because I crashed into him once and then I stole his seat and now we have to do a group project together and it's on Osmosis and I don't know anything about Osmosis, do you know anything about Osmosis?" I ask.

Brett just looks at me weirdly. "Just tell him I'm sorry and don't tell anyone you saw me," he barks. He then sprints off leaving me confused and shaken.

What is the daughter of a detective meant to do when she finds the missing person and the missing person tells her to tell the suspect that he's sorry and then tells her not to tell anyone that he saw her? I stand there confused with my heart pounding.

I need to tell someone. I quickly grab my phone and scroll through my contacts. My eyes flicker between my dad's name and that of Chase's. We had to exchange numbers for our project.

I make my decision.

He picks up on the third ring, "Look, Sage, I don't know anything about Osmosis alright?"

"This isn't about Osmosis Chase. This is about Brett Reed!" I squeak.

~~~~~~~~~~~~~~~

☆ Please vote and leave a comment ☆

Also this is the dress that Sage bought:
~~~~~~~~~~~~~~~

Chapter 12 ~ Chase

C hase's POV

"This is about Brett Reed."

Her words ring through my head and bring me to a halt. Millions of thoughts are running a rampage in my mind. How does she possibly know anything about where Brett is? No one's seen him in weeks. Suddenly I feel sick, uneasy as if someone's sent a punch to my stomach.

I close my eyes and try to control my ragged breathing.

"What on earth are you talking about Sage?" I growl out, not wanting to be messed around. If this was real then I needed to figure out what was happening, and fast.

"I errr... saw him" she sounded uneasy as well, I was probably scaring her half to death, but currently I didn't have it in me to care.

"Are you playing with me, Sage?" I demand. My blood thumps so loudly around my body, that my vision blurs.

"No I swear, but look I've got to go, there's a shop owner who I kind of ran out on......." She drifts off her voice growing quieter as she speaks. She's looking for an excuse to get off the phone. I can tell.

"Bye, I've got to go" she rushes out before the line goes dead.

I phone back her number immediately, tapping my foot against the pavement. After numerous rings, it goes to voicemail.

"Fuck," I hiss. I am an impatient person, and I need to know what was going on now. Even worse I had no clue where she was, which meant that I had no clue where Brett was either. That was frustrating me to no end.

I skim my eyes over my contacts and find who I am looking for. Perfect. I lift my phone to my ear and listen to it ring.

"Chase," his familiar voice echoes through the phone.

"Caleb," I state.

"What a pleasant surprise, never thought I'd hear from you again" his sarcastic voice rings through the phone.

"What do ya need?" he asks.

"I need you to find an address of someone for me," I say waiting for a response

"Who?" he says his interest piqued

I wasn't one to ask someone for help. I usually like to do it by myself, when you don't ask for help you don't owe anyone anything. If I've learnt anything its that its best to never be in debt to someone.

"Sage Hill," I say and listen to the silence on the other end of the call.

"The new girl in town," he says, I can tell he's confused.

"Yeah, is it possible or not?" I demand my impatience wavering, time is running out and every second I waste talking to Caleb means another second that Brett could be disappearing again.

"Yep I'll have a look and text you it when I'm done."

"Thanks," I reply and hang up.

~~~~~~~~~~~~~~~~~~~~~~~~~~~~~~~

That's it. That's the last time I'm calling Caleb to help me out. It took him over 4 hours to find one address. Was he kidding me? The world was playing a practical joke on me, I mean first Brett apparently shows up out of the blue and then when I try and find him nothing goes right.

I stalk up to the front door of the address that he gave me and knock. I wait and then the door swings open revealing Sage, she smiles and opens her mouth and then makes eye contact with me and her eyes widen, and she slams her mouth shut.

"Let's go," I say taking her hand and dragging her towards the car.

"What are you doing?" she stammers as she tumbles towards the car.

"You're taking me to where you last saw Brett," I demand.

"WHAT are you insane that's 4 hours away!" she argues. I frown, 4 hours is a long time but I wasn't about to waste a chance to try and find Brett, If I find him he can end the never-ending interviews regarding his where-abouts.

I clear my throat and nod.

"I know now get in the car Sage before I pick you up and make you come," she looks back towards the door like she wished she'd never opened it, she
~~~~~~~~~~~~~~~~~~~~~~~~~~~~~~~

then glances back at me as if she's weighing up her options. Is she thinking of running?

"Don't even think about it," I state looking her dead in the eye and watching as she glares at me and then glances at the floor.

"Fine," she mutters and reluctantly opens the passenger door and gets in. I let out a sigh and get into the driver seat and start the car.

Both of us remain silent for most of the ride other than her telling me directions when needed, I steal a glance at Sage and see her looking out the window with a small frown etched onto her face as if she's deep in thought. She glances my way as if she could tell my eyes were on her.

"We're here," I state turning off the car and looking around. It was dark, late and I didn't like my chances of finding Brett one bit.

"Errr Chase.. not to be negative or anything but I doubt Brett is still here, he seemed in a rush to leave," Sage says in a quiet voice.

At this point, I am beyond annoyed. We had come all this way to find someone that I wasn't going to be able to find because he didn't want to be found himself. I was stuck. Trapped. And by the looks of it, I wasn't going to be able to escape.

"Shit," I say as I smash my fist against the steering wheel.

"Chase its ok," she says "I can tell my dad that I saw him and that he's alive, hopefully, it'll take the pressure off you a little bit"

"Yeah and what then? He'll probably think I threatened you to say that, how convenient the detective's daughter suddenly sees the missing boy who is presumed to be murdered by me, people talk Sage they know we have been seen together in school, they will think that I forced you to back me."

Her silence fills the car and answers the question without her having to open her mouth.

"He said to tell you that he was sorry," she says her big blue eyes meeting mine. My eyes widen and my heart beats so loud that I swear she could hear it. The silence returned. I didn't know what to say. I don't think I had anything to say.

"Forget it lets just go home," I said, all too ready for this day to be over.

~~~~~~

I couldn't catch a break. I don't know what I did to deserve this. We are in the middle of nowhere and the car won't start. We are screwed. Sage looks at me her eyes wide.

"What are we going to do? We are in the middle of nowhere with a car that doesn't work. I didn't want to come in the first place!! This is your fault." She says freaking out.

I stared at her in amusement.

"Just let me phone someone to help us," I slide my phone out of my back pocket and dial a number and listen as it rings through to voicemail. But what the person says next makes me grunt in annoyance. They were closed. I mean I should have guessed it was almost 12.00 at night.

"What?" Sage asks after seeing the look on my face

"We're going to have to spend the night in the car, every place is shut," I say absorbing her reaction, she looks at me and then around the car.

"No way!" She exclaims "My dad will kill both of us if he found out where I've been all night!"
~~~~~~

"Calm down, what else can we possibly do, unless you want to try and walk home I suggest you accept it," I state. She sent a weak glare my way, but her anger was clouded by stress. I didn't like this any more than she did.

There was no denying that this was going to be a long night.

~~~~~~~~~~~~~~~~~~~~~

☆ Please vote ☆
~~~~~~~~~~~~~~~~~~~~~

Chapter 13 ~ Sage

Sage's POV

I wake at the sound of a car door shutting. I open my eyes slowly, taking in the unfamiliar environment. I'm alone in a car. Chase Rivers' car to be exact. I look out the window and see Chase leaning against the bonnet of the car as a man from a van parked across the quiet road makes his way towards us. The van reads 'car services' confirming that last night's weird sequence of events was, in fact, a reality.

I run my hand through my messy hair and look around Chase's car. The built-in digital clock reads 7 am. Shit. My dad is going to kill me. My phone died yesterday evening and in Chase's rush to find where Brett was I forgot to leave a note telling him where I was. Hopefully, he had a late night at the station and hasn't noticed my absence.

My thoughts are interrupted as the driver's seat door opens. "Morning sleeping beauty," Chase says running a hand through his always messy hair. I was too tired to even snap back. Why was he in such a good mood? We were literally stranded.

"The guy says it should only take about 20 minutes to fix the car," he says stifling a yawn. I give him a slight nod. His eyes linger on mine with an expression I can't quite read. He closes the car door and makes his way over to the man who has now opened the bonnet.

~~~~~

Half an hour later we are driving again. Chase keeps his eyes on the road but continues to glance over at me every few minutes. I lean my head on the car window.

"So what were you doing in a town four hours away by yourself anyway?" He asks, curiosity in his tone.

"Shopping for a dress for the school dance," I say.

"There's a school dance?" He asks confused, dragging his right hand through his dark hair while keeping his left hand on the steering wheel.

"Yeah, it's in a few weeks. Didn't you know?"

"Nope, been too busy becoming a suspect for murder when the alleged victim is, in fact, alive, well apparently. Are you sure it was him?" He asks, hands gripping the steering wheel firmly.

"Positive," I say. He nods. The boy was definitely Brett, I'm sure of it. It was the same boy whose face is everywhere in Mapleville. I am quick to notice how Chase accepts my answer as the truth.

"So are you going to this dance with anyone?" He asks giving me a quick glance.

"No, just my friends," I say. He nods again. A heavy silence settles in the air.

My mind flashes back to what he says about becoming a suspect. "I believe you," I blurt out.
~~~~~

He looks at me confused, a frown ever present on his face, "What?"

"I believe you don't know why Brett disappeared and well obviously that you didn't kill him because I just saw him. I don't think you're as deeply involved as everyone believes you are," I say analysing his reaction. Chase Rivers was scary but not that scary.

He doesn't respond for a while. "We use to be good friends, Brett and I. Our families were close. Brett's parents own some big business and my mum worked for them."

"What happened?" I ask, immediately regretting it. I didn't want to pressure him into telling me. He probably already didn't trust me being the detective's daughter.

But he continues, keeping his eyes ahead of him, focused on the road as if looking at the road and talking was much easier than looking at me. "My father and his mother had an affair. When Brett's dad found out he immediately fired my mum and then my dad left. That's when we stopped being friends." His green eyes were cast over.

I didn't know Chase only lived with his mother. "Oh, I'm sorry. I shouldn't have asked." Chase just shrugs.

"Do you have any siblings?" He asks, quick to change the subject away from himself.

"Nope, it's just my father and me," I say. "My mother died 6 years ago, in a car accident."

"Oh, sorry," he says.

We turn on to a much busier road. I recognise it, we must only be around half an hour away from Mapleville. I don't know whether it's the dread of my father's reaction to my absence or the now comfortable silence that has settled between Chase and I that makes me not want to leave this car.

"You're probably going to want to do a runner as soon as you drop me off," I chuckle.

"Trust me, I will," he laughs.

"Oh shit!" I exclaim.

"What?" He asks, nearly slamming on the brakes.

"Our project is due this week," I remind him. Our project on Osmosis we had failed to begin.

"You haven't done it yet?" He asks teasingly, raising an eyebrow at me.

"What do you mean I haven't done it yet? It's a group project! You are 50% of the group. I don't care if you're Chase Rivers, a group project is a group project!"

Chase just laughs, "Alright, calm down! We can go to the library some stage during the week or something. If you wanted to spend more time with me you could have just asked," He says with a smug expression on his face.

I feel my cheeks turn a light shade of red. "Need I remind you who dragged me into this car?" I retort.

"Well you called me," he says.

"You turned up at my door. Wait, how do you know where I live?" I ask suddenly confused. Maybe I was too quick to assume this boy wasn't a criminal.

"I know a guy," he shrugs.

"You know a guy who knows where I live?" I question, suddenly creeped out.

"I know a guy who knows where everyone in Mapleville lives," he says simply as if it's no big deal. I roll my eyes and look out the window.

"Hey Sage, don't tell your dad you saw Brett. Just keep it between us, okay?" He asks seriously.

Part of me is dying to tell my dad. It would help him with the case so much to know Brett was still alive. However, I know Chase is right. It could be perceived totally wrong, I don't even have evidence I saw Brett.

"Okay," I respond.

"Thanks," he says.

When we finally pull into my quiet street my heart is beating so fast. "Maybe you should drop me here," I say.

"Your house is literally right over there, don't be stupid," he says.

He pulls up in front of my house and just the sound of the car's engine causes my father to come bustling out of the house.

"Sage! Where the hell have you been? I've been calling you all morning! Why didn't you respond? Is that Chase Rivers?" He asks completely gob-smacked.

I turn to Chase, a 'told you so' look planted across my face. This situation could have been totally averted if he had just dropped me off where I had said.

"Hey Mark," he says, a sheepish grin on his face. He was making this worse.

"Sage, what the hell are you doing in a car with Chase Rivers at 11:30 am?" I can tell he's furious. I rack my brain for any possible excuse.

"Osmosis!" I exclaim. It was a pretty good excuse if you ask me but I could tell by the amused look on Chase's face and the annoyed one on my father's face that I would need to do some more explaining.

"We are doing an assignment on Osmosis, for school. It's due this week. We were at the library, researching Osmosis. Right, Chase?" I ask, giving him my best 'just go along with it' look.

"Yep, that's right," he says, flashing my father a charming grin that would have made me swoon if I wasn't so stressed about my father believing us.

"The library isn't open on Sundays," My father says, narrowing his eyes at me and Chase. Oh, how am I really suppose to lie to my father who's a detective? His job is to see through the lies!

"Well, you should have told Sage that before she left because we spent a lot of time outside the library wondering when it was going to open," Chase says so convincingly I almost believe him.

"So you're telling me you've been gone the whole morning because you were waiting for the library to open?" My father asks, sceptically.

"Well, we didn't wait the whole morning outside the library. We went into the cafe around the corner from the library and just used the internet there to research." I was impressed. His story was actually making sense. I turn to my dad and nod.

"Now I would love to chat but my mother is probably wondering where I am. Bye Sage," he says flashing me a quick smile that makes my insides flutter. What on earth was happening to me?

I don't dare look at my father until Chase's car has left. He looks puzzled on whether to believe Chase and I or not. He sighs, "I don't like that you're hanging around with that boy," he says. "He's a suspect in a criminal case," he says sternly.

"It's just for a school project Dad and besides why would he try anything against the daughter of detective whose working on his case," I try and reassure him.

At that point, it suddenly hit me that I was now much more involved in the disappearance case of Brett Reed than just being the detective's daughter.

~~~~~~~~~~~~~~~~~~~~

✰ Please vote ✰
~~~~~~~~~~~~~~~~~~~~

Chapter 14 ~ Chase

Chase's POV

There is one thought and one thought only that stands out loud and clear in my head.

What the hell is this girl doing to me?

I mean I lied to her father, the detective who's currently hunting down any evidence that I'm guilty. What if he finds out I lied to him about this. He'll probably think I'm more than capable about lying and convincing them about not knowing anything more about the location of Brett.

"Shit" I mutter under my breath as I reverse out of Sage's driveway all too eager to leave. If our lie slips up I am in deeper than I am currently, and I can't let that happen.

As I approach my house there's a looming figure standing at my door banging a fist against the wood making it shake at the hinges. I frown wondering who it could possibly be. As I park the car I jump out and slam the door behind me, making the man turn around and face me. My eyes widen, and I take another look at the man in front of me. Why the hell was Brett's dad standing on my front porch?

"Chase," He all but yells as he sets off his long strides aimed towards me.

"Where the hell is my Son! This is your fault he's gone I swear if he doesn't come back soon, You're as good as dead!" He exclaims loudly.

"I know no more than you do Mr. Reed," I say looking him square in the eyes.

I take a moment to assess him the smell of alcohol fills my senses, a frown is etched into his features as if he's spent way too long frowning at people. But it's his eyes that catch me off guard, they hold a look of emptiness to them, the passion and fire that used to be there was gone taking away the brown hue as well. They were dull. Empty.

I look down, breaking eye contact, he has lost everyone around him in the space of a few months. He is on a rampage, looking for revenge.

"You liar!" He roars as he swings his fist which collides with my face, with a sickening thud.

I look back at him, there is an urge to swing back and hit him twice as hard. But I know better. There is no point, this is what he wants. He wants me to fight back, so then he can swing the blame back onto me. They are already watching me closely I don't need this at a time like now.

He watches me, his chest rising and falling, as he stares at me with a dangerous glint in his eyes. I stare back with a stoic expression, not giving him what he wants. A reaction from me. I try and hide a wince as I feel the throb begin to expand along my cheek.

"Leave before I call the police," I threaten. And watch as he looks around and then back at me, sizing me up.

"Watch your back Chase," He says before he gets into his car and speeds away. I couldn't shake the looming feeling that this isn't over, that it isn't the last time I am going to be seeing him around. He needed someone to blame. And he had finally found that person. Me.

~~~~~~

The Sun filters into the room, making me groan as I roll over. I'm not in the mood to get up, and I sure as hell am not in the mood for school. I get out of bed and walk into the bathroom, as I look in the mirror I see that the bruise has spread like ink along my cheekbone, colouring it in a mix of blue and purple. Great. Just Great.

I zone out throughout the classes my mind is buzzing mess about Brett and his whereabouts. The teachers were talking but It was just white noise in the background of my thoughts. There are whispers about what happened to me, and why I have a bruise colouring my cheek, but I can't bring myself to give a damn.

The lunch bell rings throughout the room bringing me back to earth. There is one certain Brunette that has also consumed my thoughts alongside Brett. And I was determined to find her. She has either been avoiding me or it was a random coincidence that our paths hadn't crossed all day.

As I walk into the cafeteria a silence falls upon the room. My scowl runs along the length of the room making people turn their heads as if they find their food now to be the most fascinating thing in the room.

I don't miss one pair of eyes in particular that linger on me just a fraction longer than the rest. Of course it's Sage, she is the only person that would have the courage to do that. I shake my head and let out a chuckle, my eyes moving to meet hers. Her eyes examine my cheek and then they move to meet mine silently searching for answers. I smirk and shake my head at her and watch as one of her friends grabs her attention, giving me one last glance she turns to her friend.
~~~~~~

I walk up to her table aware that everyone is silently watching us. I stop behind her chair and watch as the few people at the table stop their conversation and stare up at me. Sage's shoulders go stiff as she turns and sees me standing behind her.

"Chase what are you doing here?" she says as blood rushes to her cheeks when she notices everyone staring, this girl is definitely not a fan of public attention.

"I need to speak with you," I say gruffly clearing my throat as my eyes wander around the girls at the table. Wishing they could just disappear, and leave Sage and myself behind.

"I errrr... okay yep," she says as she turns to get up from the table to follow me out of the room.

"No Sage it's ok, stay we need to go to the library to find some books on our assignment anyway," one of her friends rushes out giving Sage a reassuring smile.

Before Sage can object they are up and make their way towards the exit of the cafeteria. She glances back at me and gives me a small smile and gestures to the seat opposite her. I stroll around the table and take a seat.

"So, what did you need to talk about?" She says her eyes dancing everywhere but me, making me chuckle.

"How did it go with your father when you got home? Did he eventually believe you?" I ask watching her closely.

"Yeah he left it alone and didn't say much more on it," she says her eyes flickering over my bruise, she gives her head a shake as if persuading herself not to ask.

"Good," I say nodding my head "Meet me out the front of school tonight, I think its about time we finally worked on that project, don't you?" I say sending her a wink.

I watch as her eyes go wide and her cheeks once again flush pink.

"But I already told Dad I was coming straight home," she says sounding unsure.

"And I'm only free tonight sweetheart, so find a way to be there," I say giving her a smirk and turning around and making my way towards the door.

"Chase" she calls out behind me as she grips my hand making me spin around and face her.

"Yes Sage," I say my eyes staring into hers.

"I'll see you out the front," she says looking up at me.

"See you there," I say a small smile playing on my lips.

~~~~~~~~~~~~~~~~~~~~

☆ Please vote ☆
~~~~~~~~~~~~~~~~~~~~

Chapter 15 ~ Sage

- -

S age's POV

Everywhere I go there are eyes watching me and I hate it. It has been that way since lunchtime when Chase came over to my table. Well, I guess I don't blame people for being interested, it's not like seeing Chase Rivers socialise with people is a normal thing.

I don't even need to open my eyes to know that everyone is watching me as I make my way over to my desk in History. It was the last period of the day and I couldn't wait to leave to escape everyone's prying eyes.

I dump my books on the desk and look at May who's giving me her best attempt at a sympathetic look but I can tell deep down she's dying to know what happened between Chase and I at lunch. I hadn't told my three friends about Saturday or Sunday as Chase asked me to keep Brett's sudden appearance a secret.

"Ok, go for it, what do you want to know?" I ask, laughing at May who looks like she's about to burst with questions, her hazel eyes looking at me curiously.

Thankfully, by now the rest of the class is engaged in conversations and not paying me any attention.

"Are you and Chase Rivers like, you know, a thing?" She asks in a hushed tone.

"What? He literally just asked to talk to me. It's not like he got up and devoted his love for me in front of the cafeteria," I say, feeling my cheeks slightly redden.

"Yeah but it's Chase Rivers. He's doesn't exactly socialise," She says. "Seriously Sage, the whole school thinks something is going on. Not necessarily romantic, some people are worried about your safety though."

"What? You're not serious are you?" I ask. She nods, her sandy coloured hair bobbing up and down. "He just came to ask if we could work on our biology project this afternoon."

"Biology or chemistry?" She asks, raising her eyebrows at me and giving me an over exaggerated wink. I couldn't help but burst out laughing at her terrible joke.

"Would you care to tell the class what's so funny Ms Hill and Ms Hart?" Our teacher asks, standing at the front of the class not looking too thrilled.

"No sir, sorry," May quickly says. I can feel everyone's eyes once again on me and feel my cheeks begin to flush.

"This lesson I want you working from your textbooks page 240. Please do it silently," he says with emphasis on the silently part.

I sigh and open my textbook to page 240.

No matter how hard I try to concentrate though I can't stop thinking about this afternoon. I'm supposed to meet Chase outside the school to go to the library but if my Dad finds out I may as well go lock myself up in a prison cell. However, this isn't really what was taking my attention. For some reason, something has changed between Chase and I and I can't quite put my finger on it but ever since our road trip, something was definitely different. I still can't believe he opened up about his past with Brett in the car, even if it was just minor details.

I can't stop thinking about the blue and purple bruise on Chase's cheekbone. I didn't want to ask and come across as nosy but I was dying to know.

"Psst!" My thoughts are immediately interrupted. I look at May who seems to have already started her questions but is now looking at me expectantly.

"Yes?" I whisper, quickly looking at the teacher to make sure he's not looking.

"So do you like Chase?" She whispers. Just like that, I feel my cheeks begin to turn red for the hundredth time today.

"What? No of course not," I respond, trying to convince myself as well as her.

"You so do!" She giggles, her voice rising in pitch.

"Shhh!" I say rolling my eyes. Luckily, no one turns around. "I don't, I swear!" I whisper.

"Okay Sage, sure," she says smiling.

Gosh, I just wanted this period to be over!

~~~~~~~~~~~~

I shove my books into my bag and close my locker.

"Bye guys," I say to Alice, Sarah and May. Alice and Sarah give me a wave.

"Have fun studying," May says winking at me.
~~~~~~~~~~~~

"Oh shut up!" I try to look annoyed but end up laughing. Alice and Sarah look at us confused.

I pass through the hallways, people looking at me as I go. I wasn't really sure where exactly at the front of the school I was supposed to be meeting Chase. However, I didn't need to worry because he was already sitting by a tree waiting for me.

"How'd you get out so quickly?" I ask confused. He looks up at me and I couldn't help but notice his green eyes seem to brighten. However, he quickly covers it up, making me wonder if I just imagined it. By now his bruise has turned a darker shade that looks painful.

"Skipped last period," he says getting up, brushing his dark hair out of his eyes in a way that makes my heart beat a little faster. He begins walking over to his car and I jog to catch up.

As we get in the car I can no longer resist the need to know what happened to his cheek. "So, um your face," is all I say though.

He glances at me, raising an eyebrow, "Yeah I know, we can't all be blessed with these great looks." He starts the engine and gives me a wink.

"I meant the bruise," I say but it comes out sounding more like a question.

"What bruise?" He asks giving me a weird look that would have made me laugh if I wasn't so curious.

"Do you look in the mirror?" I ask. How was he oblivious to the dark colours on his cheekbone.

He chuckles, "Yes I do I just wanted to see you squirm."

Just like that, once again I become as red as a tomato. I quickly look away, "So what happened?" I ask.

"Just walked into something," he says keeping his eyes on the road.

"Bullshit," I say. As if he expects me to believe that. "You walked into someone's fist."

He doesn't say anything but I notice a hint of a smile playing on his lips.

"Well anyways thanks to you I have had the whole school stare at me as if I'm a zoo animal today," I say looking out the window at a few young kids walking home from school.

"Welcome to my world," he says almost bitterly.

~~~~~~~

The library was quiet. We find a table at the back near the non-fiction books.

I was actually pleasantly surprised, Chase was actually taking things seriously. That was until we started the bibliography and his attention was now fixated on discovering how many different ways he could annoy me. His personal favourite was throwing little bits of paper at me.

He was amused, I was not.

"Chase, seriously? We're nearly done. Find the reference for this website please," I ask, giving him my most pleading look.

"Sage, seriously? This is the most school work I've done in years, be thankful I've lasted this long," he says. Well, the boy did have a point.

I was just about to retort when I felt the all too familiar feeling of eyes watching us. Standing outside the window opposite Chase and I's table was a man looking directly at Chase. It doesn't take long for me to recognise him. I'd seen his face everywhere on TV recently. It was Brett Reed's father.
~~~~~~~

I look back at Chase who has noticed my averted attention. He looks over at the window and his eyes grow huge. He immediately stands up, fists clenched.

"Why the hell is he here?" he growls. I look back at the window and see Brett's father start to move now that he has noticed Chance looking at him. Just like that Chase is off, running through the library towards the exit.

"Chase, where are you going?" I ask, extremely confused, but he doesn't hear me as he's already out the door.

~~~~~~~~~~~~~~~~~~~~~~~~~~~~~~~~

☆ Please vote and comment ☆
~~~~~~~~~~~~~~~~~~~~~~~~~~~~~~~~

Chapter 16 ~ Chase

He is here. Standing right in front of me giving me a smug look that makes my blood boil. I clench my fists tight digging my fingers into my palm holding back the urge to throw a punch and wipe that arrogant smirk off his face.

"Hanging out with the detective's daughter, I have to say that is one way to try and get your name cleared," He says looking over my shoulder to where I'm sure Sage was watching this play out.

"Get the fuck away from us," I growl out, watching as his cool façade cracks slightly before he catches himself slipping up and glares back.

"Nice bruise," he says. My anger spikes, and right now I don't care who he is, I am one second away from storming up to him and punching him until he was out cold.

Before either of us can say anything more the door to the library swings open and Sage comes up next to my side and looks at Brett's dad, analysing him. She then turns her attention to me and smiles lightly before addressing him.

"Is there a problem here?" She asks looking at him intently. He is quick to put a kind smile on his face the last thing he needs is to get into her bad books considering who her dad is.

"No, he was just leaving," I say cutting off the conversation.

I look back towards him and give him a warning look daring him to defy me. He nods and is gone without another word.

Sage turns her striking blue eyes to me and I stare intently back at her.

"What was that all about?" She asks her eyes dancing with unanswered questions.

"Nothing," I say with a shrug of my shoulders, wanting to drop the topic already.

"That didn't look like nothing" she persists.

"It's fine don't worry just a coincidence that we were here at the same time, anyway I think we have had enough studying for today don't you think?" I say watching as she has an internal battle with herself not to fight me on it.

"Mm yeah I guess, I should probably get home soon anyway," she wavers off, glancing a look around the car park.

"Okay let's get out of here," I say strolling back into the library to collect our things and then make a beeline for the door eager to leave, thankfully Sage follows me silently her mind far away in thought.

We shut the doors to the car and I stare intently at the road in front of me, it is a silent ride for the most part.

As we pull up in front of her house I see that the lights inside are lit. Her father is home. I turn towards her and see that she s frowning at the front door as if the last thing she wants to do is get out of the car and walk up those stairs and face her dad.

"Did you tell him you were going to be late?" I ask staring down at her.

"No," she says as blood floods her cheeks. "I forgot," she mutters under her breath in embarrassment.

"Wow sweetheart were you just so eager to spend time with me that you completely forgot to tell your dad you were going to be late," I say smirking at her, making her cheeks redden even more if that was even possible.

"Whatever, bye Chase," she mutters, as she slips out of the car giving me the rude finger in the process. That girl really is something.

"Bye Sage," I say watching as her dad steps out of the front door and his eyes lock onto mine, his eyes widen for a split second before a frown forms on his face. Sending him a smirk back I drive away with a chuckle. Sage's dad was not happy, seeing me with his daughter two times in the last 48 hours. That much was clear.

Arriving home, I stroll up to the door and enter the house hurrying up the stairs to grab my bag for tonight. As I pull out the bag a photo falls from the shelves and floats down to the floor. I look down and pick it up.

It was a picture. Of Brett and myself.

We were both small and standing there with big toothless grins plastered on our faces. We were at a fair, I remember the day that was taken. Brett had wanted to go so badly, so we had pestered our parents to the point where they reluctantly had agreed. Brett had dragged me around to all the activities persisting that the specific ride or game was better than the previous. We were happy. We had sworn to each other that we would have to come back every year on the same date.

Some promises just didn't last.

I look away and scowl at the floor. Where the hell did he disappear to? He's gone and I'm dealing with all his crap. I'm getting the blame, while he's still looked upon like the good guy. I was, and still am taking the fall for Brett's problems. Every time we got into trouble when we were little I would always say it was me that instigated it. Me that came up with the idea. Brett's family cared about their reputation too much to have their son act anything less than perfect. But for me, it didn't matter I never really cared what people thought of me.

That's what drove us apart. I think Brett began believing, living and acting in his parents' fantasy world. They finally got him to be the picture-perfect son they had always wanted. It disgusted me. The fake image they put up made me sick. Brett began living a life that wasn't even his own. I wanted him to fight. He wanted to keep everyone happy. And then when the affair came out his world shattered. The blame began, and the arguments followed.

I shake my head trying to distract myself from the painful thoughts that are beginning to consume my head.

Looking at the time I realise that I am already late. Great. Aaron was not going to be happy with me. I grab my things and thump down the stairs making mum look up from what she was doing.

"Hey, where are you going?" she asks looking over the bag that is hanging over my shoulder In suspicion.

"Just out, I have to meet someone," I say giving her a small smile.

"Okay don't stay out too late, and stay out of trouble," she says lightly, leaning up to give me a light kiss on my bruise shaking her head.

"Love you," I say before turning and walking out the door.

I drive towards the warehouse. Whoever I am versing was in for it tonight. I have dealt with way too much drama in the last couple of days and I need to let off some steam.

Aaron addresses me with a firm nod of his head as he points towards the ring, a small smirk playing on his lips. I turn my attention and assess the man in front of me. He was punching the air and dancing around on his toes. I glance around the cheering crowd watching as they cheer him on as if he had already won the fight. Little did they know.

I step into the ring and my green eyes meet his blue ones. The whistle sounds around the room making people wince but turn their full attention onto us.

Let the fight begin.

~~~~~~~~~~~~~~~~~~~~

☆ Please vote ☆
~~~~~~~~~~~~~~~~~~~~

Chapter 17 ~ Sage

S age's POV

One thing is certain and that is my dad is definitely not Chase's biggest fan.

"Sage, this is two days in a row that that boy has dropped you off. What the hell is going on? How many times do I need to tell you that being around Chase is not safe. He is a suspect for crying out loud!" My dad says angrily, as soon as he closes the front door.

I honestly don't understand. What is with everyone thinking Chase is dangerous? While I haven't spent that much time with him, the hours I have spent with him have never caused me to feel as if I'm in danger.

"Dad it's a school project. It's a big part of our final grade and besides we didn't even get to pick our partners," I say, hoping he believes my little lie.

He sighs and runs a hand through his hair. I have hardly seen him in the past few weeks and I can tell he is beyond stressed about the case.

I can't sleep at night debating over whether or not I am doing the right thing by keeping Brett's sudden appearance from my dad. The police have fears they are looking for a dead body but have not yet given up on the hopes that he is still alive. I completely see where Chase is coming from though. My dad knows that I have spent time with him recently and it could end badly for Chase. Besides, what if Brett doesn't want to be found?

"Have you both nearly finished the project?" He asks, hoping my answer will be a yes so he can stop seeing Chase drop me off.

"Yes," I smile sweetly. Chase still has to finish the bibliography but he assured me he will complete it before it's due. I'm honestly so surprised that Chase did as much as he did for the project. For someone who is always late to class and never listening he seems to be quite smart.

"Did you..." he stops, debating whether or not to he should say what he wants to say. "You know I hate involving you in my work especially in a case as dramatic as this but did you notice anything suspicious about him?" He asks.

I think back to the moment Chase saw Brett's dad and stormed out of the library. But knowing that Brett's mother and Chase's father had an affair creating tension between the families explains that awkward and strange encounter.

"No, not at all. He's actually quite nice," I say giving him a shrug. He just nods his head. Knowing I am pushing my luck I ask, "So what makes you think Chase has something to do with Brett's case apart from like the fight obviously and Brett's dad suggesting him?"

"Oh don't worry about it Sage. The last thing I want is you worrying about my work when you've got your own school work to worry about," He says giving me a sympathetic look.

His phone rings at that moment and he sighs as he reaches into his pocket to answer it.

"Hello... Yes, sure I'll be there right away... Thank you, Dylan," he ends the call giving me an apologetic look. "Looks like I'll be going back to the station. But there's dinner in the fridge, just put it in the oven and I'll have some when I return." He gets up and gives me a kiss on the cheek as he goes into his study and grabs some papers.

"Don't stay up too late, it's a school night. I promise once this case is over we can go back to having our normal family dinners," he says as he rushes out the door.

Normal family dinners. Dinners haven't been normal since mum left but I get what he means. At moments like these, I wish I had a pet.

"Bye," I saw giving him a wave as he pulls out of the driveway.

I close the door turning back into my lonely house. I make my way back to the kitchen as my stomach grumbles. I look in the fridge and spy lasagne. I take it out and place it in the oven and then put a timer on for 40 minutes.

I sit on the bench as I think about everything that happened today. But mainly just about how Chase had approached me in the cafeteria and the bruise on his face which I promise myself I'll find out about later. Then there was Brett's dad. It was so bizarre that he was just standing there staring at Chase through the window. Maybe I should ask Chase about that again.

I decide that sitting here and just fossicking through my thoughts could take days at least. I get up knowing I have history homework I need to do by tomorrow.

I walk down the corridor, on the way to my bedroom when I stop at the open door of my dad's office. His office door is rarely ever open. When I say rare I'm talking about winning the lottery rare. At our old house I only ever once went into his office and that was to wake him up after he had fallen asleep the previous night.

I peek my head inside. The space is neat and tidy with a large computer sitting on his desk. There is a whiteboard with Brett's name in the centre and lots of information about him surrounding it. I've been told the saying curiosity killed the cat many times but I have no control over my feet as I find them walking over to the whiteboard.

Around Brett's name, there are details of his physical description, his family address, the date he went missing and other facts like his age and birthday. I scan my eyes across the room and nearly freak out when I notice my dad's computer is still on.

Once again I have no control over my feet as I find myself in front of the large screen. A document is already opened. It is a screenshot of someone's email draft. But not just anyone, Brett Reed. I nearly choke when I see who it is addressed to. Chase. I quickly sit down in my father's desk chair and scan my eyes along the short email.

Hey Chase,

Please meet me tonight. You know where.

It's important.

-Brett

I read over the email again and again. It is dated the day Brett disappeared and the time it was written was 5:32 pm, meaning it was after their fight in the school parking lot. However, it was never sent, just a draft.

Is this why the police are so set on the fact that Chase is playing a role in Brett's disappearance? Does Chase even know about this email? And what does Brett mean by you know where?

My phone beeps with a message making me jump out of my skin. I look at it seeing a text from Sarah.

Hey, can you send me a photo of the history homework? I forgot my book at school ☹

Right, homework. That is what I am supposed to be doing rather than snooping. I quickly get up, making sure I leave everything how I found it.

The only thought racing through my head as I make my way to my room is that Chase needs to know about this email sooner rather than later.

~~~~~~~~~~~~~~~~~~~~~~~~~~~~~~~~

☆ Please vote and comment ☆
~~~~~~~~~~~~~~~~~~~~~~~~~~~~~~~~

Chapter 18 ~ Chase

Chase's POV

What the actual fuck was going on right now?

Was the universe hell-bent on never giving me a break? My eyes angrily zero in on the numerous people beelining in and out of my front door as if they have the right to. My anger piques making me shift in my seat.

I was having an internal battle with myself about what to do. I can't help the burning feeling in my stomach that if I open this car door and proceed towards my front door the first person I see looking through my stuff is receiving a punch to the gut, uniform or not. I wasn't one who liked to share. What is mine, is mine.

My eyes flicker around the people, scanning over their meaningless grey faces until I notice one pair of deep stressed green eyes, who look as if they are about to shed endless tears. I assess her and notice the slight tremor of her hands, and with that, I am out of the car and racing towards the crowd that has gathered on the front lawn.

Mum looks up upon hearing my obvious distaste for the people around, and I notice the slight sparkle that returns upon seeing me. I muster a slightly softer look, trying my hardest to provide her with some sort of comfort.

"What the fuck?" I ask blatantly as I assess anyone who will look me in the eyes.

"Watch your language Chase," says a voice, the man stepping forward looks at me. Of course, of freaking course. Sage's dad's eyes flitter past mine and back to his clipboard which he holds firmly in his hands.

"Why are there people searching through our home?" I ask bitterly, not hiding the bite hidden beneath the words, ignoring his former remark.

"We need to search to see if there is anything related to Brett and his disappearance," a police officer adds in. Was this for real?

Was Brett ever not going to find a way to mess with my life?

"And why do you possibly think you're going to find what you're looking for here?" I state, guarded and closed, keeping my voice monotone and emotionless.

"Look, Chase, it's protocol. We have the right to look and you have to let us," Mark says assessing my reaction.

At that moment time stood still, I realise that this is never going to end, the more time that Brett spends not being found the longer the finger is going to be pointed in my direction. Nothing I can possibly say or do is going to persuade them that I am innocent, I have a history, and they have mediocre evidence but that is all they need.

I am a puppet and they have the strings. I am under their control, and that thought makes me livid.

A small hand grasps my shoulder and I turn my blazing gaze to my mother, who looks as tired as I feel, and something inside me snaps in two.

"Its fine, let them look, they have nothing to find anyway," she says her eyes searching mine.

I nod my head and hastily turn away from them all.

"I'll be back later," I mutter and hastily make my way back towards my only escape. My car.

As I drive the scenery blurs in one creating a grey blurred mess around me. My mind is far away from reality and I am more than happy to keep it there. I drive into the closest spot and jump out of the car.

Aaron's face flitters into view as I turn the corner, I almost grunt in annoyance upon seeing him. He seriously needs to give me a break, and leave me the hell alone.

"Chase," he says as his steel cold eyes meet mine.

"Yes," I say impatiently.

"Heard you are in deep in some police case," He states, looking, observing and assessing any type of reaction that I may possibly give him.

"Where'd you hear that?" I ask Aaron not playing into his hand one bit, keeping a poker face.

"I have my ways, I'm just checking that it isn't going to clash with your fighting." He's selfish, the epitome of selfish. I should have known that his first train of thought was to protect himself over anyone else.

"It won't," I state keeping my voice even.

"You better make sure of that," he counters. "And by the way you're in the ring tomorrow, it's important, don't be late," I watch as he turns, looks both ways before turning and retreating into the shadows.

I rub my hand over my eyes and let out a groan. I could not get a minute to myself lately.

"Well that was awfully interesting to watch," comes a voice from my right.

"Caleb," I state, "how did I possibly get so lucky for you to grace me with your presence?" I ask sarcastically and watch as a small smirk begins to play along his face.

"I'm just curious, as to how the almighty scary Chase Rivers is going to dig himself out of the hole he has created this time," He asks amusedly. Caleb knew how to push my buttons and right now he was doing a perfect job of it.

I wouldn't go as far as to call Caleb and me friends, but more like acquaintances. He was an outcast, but most likely by choice, as if he found life more interesting when sticking to himself, and never getting too close, or letting someone in. He remains on the outskirts and borders of society, watching and observing. And with that alone, he has gathered my respect. I have watched for too long people becoming obsessed with the idea of friends and appearing normal. Caleb caught my attention because it's almost like the thoughts of fitting in repulsed him.

And sometimes outcasts have to rely on each other from time to time.

I look Caleb up and down from head to toe, absorbing the amount he has aged since I last saw him, he is almost as tall as me. He wears a beanie, and a black sweatshirt that hangs loosely, and black jeans, he notices me staring and impatiently taps his foot, waiting for me to respond and shift the attention from him.

"Get lost Caleb," I say looking as his eyes spark with mischief.

"Now, now Chase, don't get too worked up I was just about to leave," he says toying with me. "But before I go, I wanted to ask why I didn't hear from you for months and then suddenly get a call out of the blue asking me to find a certain brunette's address?" he trails off and then his eyes meet mine again.

"But now I think I've figured it out. The suspect and the detective's daughter, what an unlikely duo, adorable isn't it?" he trails off silently laughing and he has the nerve to send me a wink.

I, on the other hand, am very far from amused.

"Caleb" I growl fed up with his games.

"I'm going, I'm going," He mutters out, flashing me a cheeky grin. "Bye Chase," he says over his shoulder as he turns and leaves.

The thing with Caleb is that when he says bye, you never know for how long you will go without seeing him. He was never one to stay in one place for too long. Never one to get attached. But he was reliable. And from time to time we needed each other.

I turn and begin walking back towards my car, my appetite completely lost.

~~~~~~~~~~~~~~~~~~~~~~~~~~~~~~~~

☆ Please vote and comment ☆
~~~~~~~~~~~~~~~~~~~~~~~~~~~~~~~~

Chapter 19 ~ Sage

S age's POV

I look up from my desk near the back of the classroom as I see Chase enter our biology room. My eyes swing to the clock perched on the wall and then gave Chase a double take as I realise the time. The boy was five minutes early.

He walks over to my desk, his dark hair a bit messier than usual and dark circles developing under his focused green eyes which are now staring into mine. His shirt is tucked out of his pants and his tie hanging loosely around his neck. The bruise running along his cheekbone is now almost faded.

"Here is the completed bibliography," he grunts, placing a sheet of papers on my desk before taking the seat next to me, dumping his books on the desk as if they were of no value.

"Nice to see you too," I say as I roll my eyes, placing the bibliography with the rest of our project.

"So did your dad crack it at you when he saw who your chauffeur was last night?" He asks with a hint of annoyance in his tone.

Deciding not to go in detail about my father's speech on the prospect of Chase being dangerous I just say, "He left soon after you. He got called into work or something," I sigh.

My dad hadn't returned until the early hours of the morning and had left before I even woke up this morning. Worrying about his health is becoming a daily habit of mine.

"Yeah he got called in to do something," he scoffs, leaning back into his chair, his hands forming fists.

"What?" I ask becoming confused. A few more people have entered the classroom but were luckily not paying us any attention.

"That something was searching my house. Head to toe. Top to bottom. Searching through all my belongings," he says, his face a clear mixture of fury and annoyance. "They didn't find anything as expected but that won't stop them from thinking that I play a fucking role in Brett's disappearance. Not just them but this whole fucking town."

Luckily, he was talking in a hushed tone or else we would be receiving a few odd glances from around the room.

"I don't think you have a role in it," I say honestly, trying to provide him with a bit of comfort.

I couldn't imagine being in his position. It's his word against everyone else's. It seems as if people have made up their opinions before being delivered all the facts. I know I don't know everything. In fact, I know quite little about the situation. But seeing Brett and the words he spoke to me make it clear that Chase is innocent.

"Wow, thanks a lot Sage! I can go back to being a normal teenager now that I know you believe I'm telling the truth," He snaps sarcastically.

Hurt immediately fills my veins. I watch him as he finally turns to glance at me. He notices my fallen expression and I don't miss the regret that fills his eyes, but he is quick to cover it. I look away from him towards the front of the classroom where our teacher is now standing. I watch as the rest of the class file in, completely aware that Chase is still staring at me as if he is unaware of what to say.

I'm on his side. I'm trying to help him. The realisation hits me then that I am working against my father in a way. I am keeping important information from him in the hopes of clearing Chase's name. Why did I care so much to help Chase though? I tell myself it's because I know he's innocent, that the police are looking in the wrong direction but deep down I know there's more to it.

Chase finally looks away from me as our teacher starts talking. I release a breath I didn't even realise I was holding.

She rambles on about our projects and how she will be collecting them. She goes over all the details she has already told us millions of times like how important this is in relation to our final grade.

Chase and I don't speak for the rest of the class. When the bell goes I quickly gather my books and race out of the room before he can say anything.

If he wants to be rude he can be rude. But that doesn't mean I am going to stick around with a first-row seat to his pity party. That sounds harsh I know but I am trying to help him and don't want to put up with him if he is going to be a dick.

The next three classes leave me bored out of mind by the time the lunch bell sounds. I walk to my locker slowly, most kids already making their way to the cafeteria. I open my locker and shove my folders into it, all hopes of remaining an organised student destroyed. I grab my lunch, some leftover lasagne from last night and go to close my locker when I feel someone's eyes on me.

I turn around. The green eyes of Chase flash with uncertainty as he approaches me. I raise an eyebrow at him, letting him know I haven't forgotten his snappy remark.

He clears his throat, "Um can we uh talk?" I can tell by his face that he is feeling bad about what he said in biology.

"Sure," I say. His green eyes brighten a little bit as he turns around and starts walking away.

What the hell is he doing? I thought he wanted to talk.

He turns around noticing I haven't moved from my spot, "Are you coming or not?" he asks. I close my locker and begin to follow him. We exit the school building and he leads us to a stretch of grass under a large tree.

He sits down and looks up at me expectantly, "Are you going to take a seat or just stand there forever sweetheart?" He asks, a hint of a smirk playing on his lips. Well, his confidence has returned.

I roll my eyes and sit down next to him, "You wanted to talk?" I ask, noticing how close we are sitting.

"Yeah, I just wanted to um apologise I guess for um what I said earlier today," He says rubbing his hand along the back of his neck.

Now it is my time to smirk, "What is happening? The big, bad Chase Rivers is apologising to me? Wow, am I dreaming right now?" I ask, feigning disbelief.

"Did you just admit to dreaming about me Sage Hill? Oh, imagine if your dad found about that!" He says, his signature smirk present on his face.

"Ha! You wish I dream about you," I retort. My phone chimes preventing him from making another comment.

I look at the screen and the smile I didn't realise I was wearing disappears from my face.

Hey Sage, another long night for me tonight. Won't be home until midday tomorrow. Love you x

"What's wrong?" Chase asks, noticing my change in emotion.

"Oh it's just my dad," I say, "He won't be home until tomorrow. Another lonely night for me," I laugh bitterly.

I understand he is busy and I probably sound like a spoilt teenager but he is the only family member I have left. It has happened before where my dad gets so involved in a case he completely forgets he has a life he needs to live.

Chase gives me a sympathetic look, "You can come to my house and have dinner with my mum and I tonight if you want that is. Just so you don't have to be lonely."

I can't ignore the warm fuzzy feeling that fills my stomach as those words exit his mouth.

"Your mum wouldn't mind?" I ask.

"No, not at all. She would probably like some more company," he shrugs.

"Alright, thank you," I smile.

"Come around at 5 pm," he says and takes my phone, writing his address in.

"See you then," I smile.

~~~~~~~~~~~~~~~~~~~~~~~~~~~~~~~~~~~
~~~~~~~~~~~~~~~~~~~~~~~~~~~~~~~~~~~

☆ Please vote and comment ☆

Chapter 20 ~ Chase

C hase's POV

What was wrong with me?

Had I actually just offered for Sage to come to my house. This wasn't me. Never had been. I am not one to play the nice guy. That was Brett's job. Not mine.

I don't do feelings. Never have.

But I couldn't shake the nagging feeling eating up my spine when she said she was spending the night alone again. I didn't like the look on her face, it made my stomach churn. And had resulted in me speaking without thinking.

I focus my whirling mind back onto the road as I turn into my driveway. I take note of the light that that comes filtering through the small window off the kitchen.

Here goes nothing.

I stroll into the house and make my way to the kitchen and open the fridge, grabbing out a bottle of water. Mum's attention snaps to me almost immediately.

"Hi honey, I was just going to start preparing dinner," she says looking up at me.

"Ok," I mutter out before glancing at the living room then back at her.

"Actually mum, we are going to have company tonight with dinner," I say watching as I now suddenly attain mum's full attention. Exactly what I didn't want.

"What, who?" she asks, trying to hide the slight excitement hidden underneath her tone. I can't help the small smile that begins to form on my face at the fact that she was getting excited over this.

"Just a girl from school," I state trying to cut the conversation off, but my hope is short-lived as her smile grows larger by the second.

"Really? What's her name?" She asks rocking back and forth on her toes. She is never going to let this go.

And I am completely regretting the invitation now.

"Mum," I say sternly, trying to leave the room before the conversation eventuates any further than it already has.

A light patter drums against the door vibrates through our small house. Sage has arrived, and I can't help but frown at the fact that my heart beats slightly faster than usual. What the heck?

Before my mind has time to function my mum beats me to the door and swings it open revealing a slightly stunned Sage. I look at both of them and them and then turn towards Sage and watch as her blazing blue eyes meet mine.

"Hi, nice to meet you Ms Rivers," Sage says flickering her vivid eyes back onto my mum.

Mum is quick to respond "Hi....." She looks up at me to fill the blank of her name, but Sage beats me to it.

"Sage, Sage Hill," she says quietly, her eyes meeting mine once again.

I, on the other hand, am absorbing my mum's reaction, her eyes flash with recognition, and she is quick to look towards me in confirmation. I give her a look to say drop it, and she focuses her attention back onto Sage.

"It's so lovely to meet you, please come in," she says. They turn and make their way to the kitchen, just as I begin to follow them a buzz in my pocket halts my steps.

With a grunt, I pull it out and watch as Aaron's name flashes across the screen.

Why was he calling me right now?

I notice that Sage has stopped also, she looks up and her eyes dash around my face soaking up and traces of my frown. She isn't one to miss much.

"Everything okay?" she asks her eyes flashing down to my phone which I hold tightly in my hand.

"Peachy," I mutter out. "I'll meet you in the kitchen, just let me take this call," I state before turning around and walking down the hall and turning the corner.

"What?" I say not caring that it may come across as rude.

"Where the fuck are you?" an angry voice comes scorning from the other end of the phone.

"What?" I mutter out again, annoyed and now confused.

"Don't what me. You have a fight tonight and are nowhere to be seen!" He states in a rushed tone. Shit. How did I honestly manage this? I had completely forgotten.

I am fucked.

There is no way I am getting out of this house at the moment with Sage and my mum around the corner.

"Look kid you better be here within the next 30 minutes or you're done," he states, and then the line goes dead. Shit.

I smash my hand into the wall in frustration. And hear small footsteps before Sage's head pokes around the corner, a confused and slightly bewildered look on her face.

"Ummm... Chase?" Her unanswered questions linger in the air, but she decides against asking me.

"Yes?" I say keeping my tone even, we didn't need a repeat of this morning again. I decide to turn this conversation in a different direction and deflect it from me.

"As lovely as it is standing here and talking to you sweetheart, I'm hungry and I bet you are too so let's go," I say turning and all but dragging her to the dining room.

We enter, catching my mum's attention, but she is quick to divert it back to what she was previously doing.

"Dinners ready," she says and both Sage and I follow her to the table. This was one of the first meals I had sat down to eat in weeks, and I could tell by the way mum was smiling softly she was happy.

"It looks lovely," Sage says as she slips into the nearest seat.

I quickly decide to take teasing her to one step further.

"You do know that's my seat," I say and watch as this time she glances at me and rolls her eyes, sticking her tongue out at me.

"Well too bad, its mine now," she says cheekily.

I let out a laugh and drag another seat over. I don't miss how my mum watches our exchange with a confused face.

The next 20 minutes is spent with me glancing every so often at my watch as I painfully watch the seconds bleed into minutes. I am sure Sage has picked up on the nervous bounce of my knee under the table, she has either chosen to ignore it or is probably planning to confront me on it another time. Knowing Sage she will probably go with the latter option.

As soon as the conversation begins to die, Sage informs us that she must be getting home. I stand and hold my hand to the small of her back as I walk us towards the door, not before mum repeats that she must come over again.

Sage looks up at me her eyes soft, "Thanks for tonight," she says glancing around taking in the details of the house.

"No problem, Goodnight Sage," I say watching as she turns and leaves. A small smile plastered on her face.

I glance back at the clock once she is gone. I need to leave, and now if I want any chance of making it to Aaron in time.

And with that in mind, I race out of the house, usher a quick goodbye to my mum and make my way towards my car.

~~~~~~~~~~~~~~~~~~~~~~~~~~~~~~~~~

☆ Please vote and comment ☆
~~~~~~~~~~~~~~~~~~~~~~~~~~~~~~~~~

Chapter 21 ~ Sage

S age's POV

I make my way to my dad's car which he thankfully isn't using tonight. I don't need to turn around to know Chase is still standing at the door watching me.

I look back at Chase's house before getting in the car and starting my drive home. His place is very different from mine. While his single storied house is a lot smaller than my double storied house, his obtains a feeling of comfort and love, unlike my lonely, empty house, something shifts inside me as I take note of that.

I turn the radio up loud as I drive home, a Rihanna song playing. As I pull into my driveway I can't help the sinking feeling in my stomach. I wish I was back at Chase's house, where warmth would engulf me.

I close my car door and make my way to the front door. I unlock it and enter my dark household. I turn on the lights and go to the kitchen. The only thing I feel like right now is tea. Nice, warm tea, to replace a feeling of warmth that this house is currently lacking.

I make my tea and then go sit on the couch. My mind flitters back to the weird day I had today.

First, Chase and I had a mini argument. Looking back I don't blame him for snapping at me. It must have been so invasive having so many people search his house but I guess the fact that they didn't seem to find anything is reassuring.

Then, he approached me at my locker wanting to talk so he could apologise. Chase didn't seem like the kind of guy that apologises so the rarity of the situation had made my heart flutter.

Surprisingly, he then invited me back to his house for dinner. I was beyond grateful for that, the last thing I had wanted was to come home to an empty house.

Ms Rivers was very nice. I could tell the mentioning of my last name had fazed her and I had instantly regretted saying it. However, she was very nice and welcoming. She looks a lot like Chase, very similar green eyes but a lighter shade hair colour, more of a light brown colour.

When Chase had left to take a call from god knows who, we had made small talk. She asked me about school and I asked her about work, she seemed uncomfortable when asked, but was quick to respond. She is currently unemployed but is looking for a job. Our conversation was interrupted when I heard a bang.

I immediately went to explore finding Chase with his fist in the wall. Must have been a bad phone call then. It left him on edge for the rest of the evening. He sat beside me with his knee bobbing up and down as if he were agitated and ready to jump up and leave.

His mum seemed to notice this to but didn't press him for information. I decided to add it to my list of 'Things I need to ask Chase.'

So far my list looks like this:

- How did your cheek get bruised the other week? (because you certainly didn't walk into something)

- Why did Brett ask me to tell you he was sorry?

- Is there a reason apart from family history that Brett's dad was just staring at us in the library?

- Who called you before dinner?

- Why did you punch a hole in the wall?

- Why were you so agitated during dinner?

I guess you could say I am a curious person.

I wish there was a way that I could help Chase to clear his name. If only Brett would return and tell everyone he's alright and Chase has nothing to do with his disappearance.

But is Brett really alright?

When I saw him he looked quite dishevelled and tired but he didn't look like he had been harmed. No one else was around monitoring him so maybe he left on his own free will? But why would he want to leave?

From what I had heard his life seemed pretty put together. He was Mr Popular with a fan base to prove it. Captain of the footy team with good grades and a good personality to match it.

So what is he running away from? Or who?

I realise I had completely forgotten to inform Chase about Brett's email draft I found last night. I make a mental note to tell him tomorrow at school.

I get up, my head pounding with unanswered questions. I make my way towards my bedroom but find myself standing outside my father's office. The door is closed today but that doesn't stop my ambition as my hand grabs the doorknob, turning it.

I am honestly surprised my father doesn't put a lock on his door. I guess he trusts me not to be a snoop. Maybe he should reconsider that thought.

I don't know what I'm looking for but I just feel the need for some validation. That maybe it is possible that Brett has run away on his own accord.

Most information regarding the case is at the police station and I'm not going to even consider breaking in there. My dad is extremely dedicated to his work tends to bring things home so he can work over hours.

I spy a folder tucked away in the corner and make my way over to it, curiosity sparking through my veins. I open it and find a report titled 'Disappearance Date.'

I find brief details outlining the sequence of events of Brett's disappearance:

4 pm – Fight in the school car park with Chase Rivers, a small crowd gathers, no one knew what it was about.

4.15 pm – Brett leaves the scene, Chase already gone

5 pm – Arrives home, father and mother both present, Brett does not say much but seems bothered by something according to Mrs Reed.

5.30 pm – Parents leave to attend a meeting regarding work.

5.32 pm – Brett writes an email draft addressed to Chase but does not send.

6 pm – Parents return and Brett is nowhere to be found. Try contacting him but left his phone at home. No items of value seem to be missing.

7 pm – After an hour of searching parents alert police. Police search starts.

I turn the page. I don't know what I am looking for but I can't stop my eyes from searching nonetheless.

This page is a report on Brett's room. I see a fingerprint test has been taken on things like doorknobs, his phone, bed etc. However, the tests came back giving no fingerprint identity but Brett's and his parents'. This is similar to the fingerprint tests taken around the rest of the house.

I guess this means if the police think he was abducted, he certainly wasn't taken from his house. Or maybe he left with nothing but the clothes on his back to make a runner. I wonder if the police have even considered that theory. But maybe they have and they just think the possibility of him still being alive is slim.

I saw him over two weeks ago so how do I know if he is even still alive. Shit. What if he is dead? What if I was the last person to see him? What if having told my dad weeks ago could have saved him?

I curse myself. I don't know if he is alive or not. I need to stop worrying about my part in this because I bet my dad will find him soon and everything will be alright. Chase can go back to being a normal teenager, well as normal as Chase Rivers can be considered. I can go back to worrying about things like homework.

Shit homework. I close the folder and leave his office. Homework is what I need to be focusing on right now.

~~~~~~~~~~~~~~~~~~~~~~~~~~~~~~~~

☆ Please vote and comment ☆
~~~~~~~~~~~~~~~~~~~~~~~~~~~~~~~~

Chapter 22 ~ Chase

C hase's POV

My head thumps with adrenaline. My blood pumps around my body, creating a light humming feeling to course through my veins.

I need to focus.

I turn my adverted attention back onto the man in front of me. He throws his hands around in the air, causing the crowd to play into his actions and cheer louder as a result. He's cocky. He thinks he has already won the fight.

We begin to dance around the ring circling each other in the process. I doge his punches and kicks and he does the same. I take note of the fact that his attention often wavers, he gets distracted easily. This, I could use to my advantage. I send un unexpected punch his way and it makes a sickening thud as it connects with the side of his face, he frowns in reply and I smirk back.

Just as I set up to send a kick his way, my eyes unintentionally meet a certain pair of dark brown eyes, and my heart comes to a complete and utter stop.

I'm going to choke.

Scratch that I'm going to vomit.

This can't be happening.

I'm delusional. I have to be.

My blood runs cold and my hands become clammy. What the fuck was Brett doing here?

I don't notice until too late that my opponent has picked up on my adverted attention and sends a fist hurtling towards my face, and a kick to my side. They are certainly going to bruise, and as I notice the slight thump under my cheekbone I know that it already is.

I snap my attention back to him, reluctantly taking my eyes off Brett. I am afraid that if we break eye contact, he will leave, disappear into the shadows and become a figment of my imagination. And I couldn't let that happen.

I faintly hear Aaron screaming out my name in the distance, telling me to snap out of it, and focus. I can't. I've forgotten how to breathe. The guy in front of me has got me beat. And right now I can't bring myself to care. I must get out of this ring. I have to see Brett.

"Time Out," I recognise Aarons' voice. The fight is over. He is mad. Livid. This was an important fight for him, for his reputation, and I blew it.

"What the fuck was that?" He states silently seething at me as I jump out of the ring.

"I need to go, I'll be back," I state shoving past him.

Brett's head is now turned and heading towards the door. There is no chance in hell I am letting him leave without talking to him. And I sure as fuck aren't going to let Aaron stand in my way.

"Wait! Chase!" He yells after me. But it's too late, I'm already turned and running out the door after Brett.

I run through the door and almost smash into the person standing on the other side.

Brett, he was here, but he also isn't. He looks drained and tired. His brown eyes dark and guarded. He looks like a fragment of what he used to be. He has rough sadness to his features.

We both stand in silence. After all this time, I don't know what to say to him. His hooded eyes meet mine. I am completely rooted to the spot as if the cement has grown up from the ground and has grabbed my feet with a steel grasp.

He looks as if he has something to say, unlike me, who has suddenly become mute. I feel like I am seeing a ghost.

He notices my expression and a flash of guilt passes through his brown eyes, as he shifts his gaze.

"Look I can't be here, but I wanted, no needed to say sorry," He says.

Is he for real? A sudden rush of anger spikes deep within me causing a flame.

All the anger floods back into my body filling me from bottom to top.

"What the fuck?" I seethe as I stare him dead in the eyes. I was now wrathful. I reach my hands out and shove him. Hard. Making him rock on his feet to regain his balance.

"You left," I state my voice remaining stoic and emotionless.

"You don't understand! I had too," he says, pleading with me to understand. I understood, or at least I used to.

I take the time to notice how broken he truly looks, the bags under his eyes are dark and prominent. He didn't understand that when he up and left something inside me snapped. He was escaping his reality, but I would never be able to escape mine.

He has made my reality worse, to make his better.

He is drowning me in order to stay afloat.

And now I am seeing red.

How dare he leave and let everyone believe it is my fault.

"You screwed me over in order to save yourself, Brett," I say watching as he absorbs my words, hiding a wince.

"I'm sorry, did she tell you what I said?" He asks referring to Sage. He is pleading with me. Trying to gain my forgiveness.

"Leave her out of this," I snarl back at him.

"I'll make it right. I just need more time," he replies.

"You better be able to find a way to get me out of this shit, or so help you, Brett, I will come and find you and drag you back to Mapleville myself," I say.

"I can't go back!" he states. "I don't want to see them again, I can't continue to live like that," He says.

He had finally cracked.

His parents' pressure had finally broken him.

"Find a way to fix this," I growl out "Because soon I'm going to be behind bars for something that I never did."

I watch as recognition flickers across his face before he focuses on something behind me.

"I will make sure that doesn't happen," He says, his voice filled with a silent promise.

"Bye Brett," I say, not knowing what to say back to him, and I turn and make my way towards my car deciding that it is a better idea than returning inside to face Aaron's anger.

I also notice the bruise covering my cheek has grown and expanded along my face. Shit. There is no way I can go home like this. I need to clean up before I can possibly face my mum. So I start the car and head to one of the last places I would have ever thought about going a couple of weeks ago.

Sage's house.

I arrive there not long after being in the car and get out, heading towards the front door. Deciding against knocking, in case she is asleep, I decide to ring.

She picks up on the third ring.

"Chase?" She asks uncertainly.

"I'm outside sweetheart, so please hurry before I freeze to death," I say, smiling as I hear her response.

"What?" she all but yells through the line. "Why are you here at 12 in the middle of the fucking night!?" she demands.

I chuckle in response, and before I can respond the line goes dead, and I hear a small number of footsteps towards the door before it swings open revealing Sage, standing in small shorts and a large jumper, with her hair wrapped securely on the top of her head in a knot. I can't help but acknowledge that my heart stops a little upon seeing her.

I glance around, before meeting her eyes.

"So are you going to invite me in or..." I trail off watching as a blush coats her cheeks.

~~~~~~~~~~~~~~~~~~~~~~~~~~~~~~~~~~

☆ Please vote and comment ☆
~~~~~~~~~~~~~~~~~~~~~~~~~~~~~~~~~~

Chapter 23 ~ Sage

S age's POV

"So are you going to invite me in or..." Chase trails off.

I feel my cheeks go red as I realise I'm only wearing a pair of PJ shorts and a jumper as well as my hair tied up in a messy bun. I feel his eyes scan me over from head to toe.

My embarrassment is short lived as I take in his face. His face that had only just recovered from bruising is once again a shade of purple, this time on his opposite cheekbone. This wound, however, looks worse than the previous. He looks tired with dark circles developing under his eyes.

"Oh my gosh, you're face!" I exclaim, opening the door wider, letting him in.

He gives me a thankful smile that makes my heart beat quicken. I don't fail to notice how he winces when he moves as if each step is more painful than the last.

"Sage we've already been over this. I can't help that I was blessed with these god-like looks. Surely you should be used to it by now," He says giving me a wink.

I roll my eyes, "Glad to see your ego isn't as damaged as your face." He just chuckles. I close the door behind him, thanking the heavens my dad isn't home to witness Chase stepping foot in this house.

He looks around at the corridor enveloped in darkness. I flick on a light, ushering him into the nearby bathroom where first aid supplies are likely to be. Only in the light do I take in the extremity of the bruise spread across his cheek.

I feel his eyes on me, watching me assess his face. "Well we need to clean this up," I state, avoiding eye contact due to the proximity in which we are standing.

"Aren't you going to ask me how this happened?" He asks sounding confused. I lift my gaze to meet his. His dark hair is a mess as per usual and his green eyes focusing solely on my blue ones.

"First I'm going to clean up your face and then you're going to tell me what happened," I say dragging him over to the vanity where I begin rummaging through drawers.

He positions himself so he is leaning on the vanity, he winces as he adjusts his weight. "What? Where else are you hurt?" I ask, not being able to hide the worry in my tone.

"Don't worry about it, you've already done enough," He says, his green eyes still watching my every move.

"Don't be stupid Chase! You're hurt," I say standing to meet his gaze. I cross my arms, letting him know there is no way in which he won't tell me.

He watches me for a few seconds before taking his jacket and off and lifting his black t-shirt up to reveal his tan skin. A long bruise runs up his left side as if he had been kicked in the ribs. His skin had broken and even though the injury is recent it is already the shades of blues and greens. I find my eyes scanning the rest of his bare skin and my cheeks immediately redden as I take in his sculpted abs. I quickly look back to his wound.

"Enjoy the view sweetheart?" He asks with a smirk on his lips.

"What the fuck happened to you, Chase?" I ask ignoring his comment.

"Well it's a long story," he sighs.

"Well, then you better get explaining," I say as I take out the first aid kit to begin attending to his wounds.

I try to prevent my already red face from turning an even darker shade as he removes his shirt so I can start with that injury.

"Just promise you won't tell your dad or like anyone," He asks sternly absorbing my reaction to his words closely. I look into his eyes, now full of seriousness and I find myself nodding.

He rubs a hand over his face as if he can't believe he is actually telling me this.

"My family obviously isn't the wealthiest and money has always been a problem, even when my dad was still around. A few years ago I decided I wanted to help. I had been approached by an older kid at school who had watched me fight with another dude at lunch once. Don't ask me why we were fighting because I honestly don't remember. Anyways this guy said he knew a place where I could go to improve my fighting and fight others for money. I didn't even consider it to begin with. I didn't want to make getting into fights a frequent occurrence but one night my mum and dad had this huge fight about money. I just remember sitting in my bedroom and thinking how can I put an end to this?" His green eyes flicker with pain as he reminisces on the fight, but he is quick to cover it up.

"So I approached the guy at school the next day and he gave me all the details. He hooked me up with a manager who organised some fights for me. I was shit, to begin with. I didn't begin winning until weeks later, but I was determined and never gave up. Mum found out though and was furious. So was Brett. Luckily, she never told dad or I would have been in deep shit. When we found out about Dad's affair, she begged me to stop. I didn't want to, not because I was addicted but because we needed the money then more than ever. But I stopped anyway because mum felt like she was losing both of us simultaneously." He winces as I run a cotton pad over his wound, trying to clean it.

I can't believe Chase started illegal fighting at such a young age to earn money for his family. I couldn't imagine what he had had to endure.

"I hated fighting with a passion. Still do," He sighs running a hand through his hair. He gazes off into the distance as if he is stuck in another world. "But mum has been unemployed for months, seems like nobody wants to employ the suspect's mother. Money was at a new time low and I didn't know what to do so I went back. Even though I'd been away for over a year as soon as I stepped into the ring everything came back to me. Since going back I haven't lost a fight. Well, that is until tonight," He says painfully.

"What happened?" I ask. My voice seems to bring him back to reality, snapping him out of his trance.

"Brett was there," He says eyes blazing with anger.

"What?" I choke out.

"He was there, watching the fight. It threw me completely off guard and I just couldn't do it," He says sighing helplessly.

What? Why was Brett watching Chase's fight? Well, at least it means he is still alive.

"Did you talk to him?" I ask, my voice coming out strained.

"Yeah, I ran out and confronted him. I don't even remember what was said. It's all a blur. But I definitely got mad at him. I remember he said he was sorry and he was trying to fix it but he couldn't go back. Couldn't go back to his family," He sighs rubbing the back of his neck.

"What do you mean he couldn't go back to his family?" I ask, looking up at Chase.

"His parents were obsessed with image Sage. Still are. They always wanted him to be the perfect kid, no mistakes allowed, perfect grades only. His mum was nice but his dad was terrible. After the affair, it only increased in severity. Brett's dad feared his life was falling apart. He went out of his way to ensure the three of them appeared the same happy family they had always been to the public eye. The affair broke Brett and I's friendship but the need for perfection that that family had is what really destroyed it, shattering it at the core. His dad never liked me because I brought out the real Brett," he shrugs. His face is blank, trying to hide any sign of emotions but I can feel deep down that he is still sad, hurt and mad.

I reach out to him, placing my hand on his arm and giving it a squeeze.

He turns his head to me but before either of us can do anything I hear a familiar sound. The sound of my father's keys in the front door. My eyes widen with alarm. He said he wouldn't be home until later the next day. I guess it technically is the next day but 1 am isn't my idea of late.

I grab Chase's arm, pulling him out of the bathroom, making sure to turn the light off as I go. I drag him into my room just as I hear the front door swing open. I quickly and quietly close my door. I look at Chase's face.

For once the boy looks slightly worried, probably at the thought of getting caught.

"Hide in there," I whisper. "Don't make a sound and don't come out until I tell you to."

I don't even wait for a response before shoving him into my wardrobe and diving into my bed. Not daring to make a sound as I hear my dad shuffle around in the kitchen.

~~~~~~~~~~~~~~~~~~~~~~~~~~~~~~~~~

☆ Please vote and comment ☆
~~~~~~~~~~~~~~~~~~~~~~~~~~~~~~~~~

Chapter 24 ~ Chase

Chase's POV

Before my mind can function and register what she's doing the door shuts in my face, leaving me staring after her. What the hell is going on? Thank god I parked down the street to her house, or I would have been busted before he even set foot in the house.

This girl is slowly driving me insane.

I tune in and listen as I hear a soft thud, which must be Sage leaping into her bed. I almost chuckle at the thought. But the last thing I needed currently is to get caught shirtless in the detective's daughters' room right now. Shit, how did I end up in this situation?

My mind is fuzzy, filled with a haze. I rub my hand over my face trying to regain my thoughts back in order. Seeing the pure and utter worry in her blue eyes as she looked at my cut, made something in my stomach churn. I wasn't used to letting people in enough to care about me, but seeing how worried she was, made my chest ache. And when she blushed and nervously glanced away as she looked at my body makes her even more fucking adorable.

Shit what was happening to me?

The sound of footsteps lightly tapping up the hall catches my attention almost immediately. The sound of Sage's dads voice filtering into the room, and the words that come out of his mouth make my mind run blank.

"He was seen? Are you sure it was him?" he asks, there is an edge to his voice, that makes me feel unsettled.

There is a silence that follows, and every second becomes an hour as I strain to hear.

"Well that changes everything," he states keeping his tone quiet.

"Ok, yes I guess, ok I'll be there in 10," he says before I hear the footsteps retreat towards where they had originally come from.

Did this guy ever sleep?

The sound of the door shutting once again is all it takes before the wardrobe door is swung open, and a wide-eyed Sage assesses my face, not daring to glance down at my bare stomach.

"Well that was interesting," I state, and she nods her head along in a silent agreement.

"Yep," She says popping the p, her mind far away. A small frown begins to form amongst her soft features, and I almost feel the need to reach out and smooth the skin along her forehead to make the lines disappear.

"Sage," I mutter out catching her attention. "What's going on inside that mind of yours that has you frowning?" Her bewildered eyes flash to mine in a daze.

"Err.. nothing, but we must clean up your bruise before the swelling gets worse," she says taking my hand lightly in hers and leading me back to the bathroom.

"Sit," she commands as she leans back down to the drawers that are still slightly open from 10 minutes ago when we had been in here.

"Chase, I have been thinking of the right time to mention this but I found an email in my dad's office from the night that Brett went missing, and it was addressed to you but was never sent," she says hesitantly.

"What did it say?" I ask, keeping my voice low, trying to hide how curious I suddenly am.

"To meet him, and that you would know where, but it was never sent, so he must have changed his mind," She trails off, watching me closely.

I know where he would have meant, we had climbed a tree one night and talked about running away. Escaping to a place far better than our realities, we had sat and mapped out a plan, of what we would do and how we would do it. We had sworn that we wouldn't leave the other behind. That we would start over, in a new city, a country even, create new versions of ourselves, better and finally be free. Free, the word is bitter to me now.

He was thinking of asking me to join him.

But why?

If there is one thing Brett has taught me it is that promises are made to be broken.

"Chase," Sage's voice splits my memory in half, focusing my attention back to her I notice that she is now leaning in front of me, leaving those all too tempting legs on display.

"It's fine. It's going to work out, we will find a way to fix this," She says turning her attention back to my bruise as she rubs something lightly onto it.

Funny, in the space of a couple of hours two people have promised me they would help find a way to get me out of this mess.

It seems that currently, everyone is so hell-bent on helping me, but I'm not so sure I am willing to accept the help in return.

I am confused, and I have no clue what I am going to do.

I turn my attention back to Sage.

I take note of the fact that she is now sitting closer to me and her face is mere inches from mine, and I can't help the warm feeling that courses through me at having her this close. Her breathing slowly becomes uneven as she tenses. Her bright observing eyes meet mine, and my chest tightens as my eyes flicker across the features of her face, before focusing on her lips. They are screaming to be kissed. Without thinking I lift my hand and lightly brush my knuckles along her cheek, neither of us notice that we have both unthinkingly leaned in, and now our lips are centimeters away from touching. I acknowledge the slight sparks that erupt within me from having her lips slightly brushing against mine.

Fuck.

I've dug myself in too deep and I have no clue how I'm going to get out. The feeling that is starting to become constant whenever Sage is around is becoming addicting, and I can't help but think that I don't want it to end.

The sound of vibrations make Sage break away from the kiss and look up at me, her eyes are clear, bright and solely focused on me. I don't look away. I don't think I ever want to, and that thought is scaring the shit out of me right now. Whatever just happened couldn't be undone. We have crossed a line that can't be backtracked.

What the fuck is happening to me?

I clear my throat to break the trance that has sucked us under and is keeping us locked in a daze that I'm not sure I want to end.

"Chase," she says. She's waiting for me to say something, and right now my mind is running blank. I don't know what to say. And I sure as hell don't know what happens next.

I don't kiss people, with a meaning hidden behind it. This isn't me. I am well and truly in over my head. But I can't discard the feeling that ignited within me as her lips had touched mine.

"Sage," I say. I'm completely lost and don't possibly know what to say, usually, I was the one in control, but right now I had no clue what to do.

"What happens now?" she asks lightly, her unanswered questions filling the room.

"I have no idea," I say back.

"It's late and definitely too late for you to leave and drive at this time," she says, glancing down at the watch on her wrist. "Just stay here tonight, and we can figure it all out tomorrow," she says, turning and walking towards her room.

I take a moment to gather my thoughts before following her. I don't do feelings, and right now I feel slightly nauseous.

Walking in, the tension is thick in the air, it is suffocating me, and I can't take it much longer.

"If you wanted me to sleep in your room you could have just asked sweetheart," I say sending her a wink and watch as she turns from where she is headed, the bathroom to send me the rude finger over her shoulder.

I let out a chuckle as she returns to the room before turning her attention to me, carrying a blanket and pillows.

"You're injured, so you're in the bed," she says leaving no room for arguments, but I was quick to rebut.

"No way," I state "You get in the bed, I'll take the floor, and if you even try and open that pretty little mouth of yours to argue, I will pick you up, injured stomach or not and put you on the bed myself," I finish flashing her a look as if to say I'm not kidding.

"Mmmk" she grumbles, after deciding it was better not to argue and find out I wasn't lying about my earlier statement.

And with that I lie down and settle myself onto the hard ground, shifting and holding in a grunt of pain, trying to escape.

And I let sleep slip me under, and for the first time in months, I let my body relax.

~~~~~~~~~~~~~~~~~~~~~~~~~~~~~~~~

☆ Please vote and comment ☆
~~~~~~~~~~~~~~~~~~~~~~~~~~~~~~~~

Chapter 25 ~ Sage

S age's POV

What the fuck just happened?

Did Chase and I really just kiss?

This can't be happening. Shit. Shit. Shit.

It all happened so quickly. We were so close. He lifted his hand and brushed my cheek, creating my pulse to quicken. His gaze was soft and tentative. My heart was beating a million miles per minute. At that moment I knew there was nothing I wanted more than his lips on mine.

His lips were soft and as soon as they met mine fireworks erupted inside me. I have never felt this way before and the feeling alone is starting to scare me.

I think back to all the moments we have spent together over the last few weeks. Moments where I could have sworn he had hated me. But we were always flirting. Even if we didn't realise it at the time. As the weeks passed he began to open up more and more to me. And then tonight. Tonight, he really opened up.

I couldn't believe how much he told me about his childhood and fighting. I could never even imagine being in his position. And yet he decided that I was someone worth telling. Someone worth spending time with.

I turn my gaze to where Chase is sleeping on the ground in my bedroom. I can tell by his deep breathing he is asleep. Good, he needs the rest.

What if it was just in the moment though? We were close and it was late. What if it's just a pointless kiss to him? I can't help the pain that runs through my heart as I even consider that thought. I don't want it to be a meaningless kiss to him because I know it definitely wasn't meaningless to me.

The kiss was interrupted by his phone buzzing. I can't help but wonder what would have happened if it had never buzzed. Would we be in even deeper over our heads then we are currently?

Thank god my dad had left again. I don't even know why he returned home to begin with but what I overhead on the phone just shone a light on the truth of Chase's story. Brett had been seen on the outskirts of town tonight. Chase had also seen him. If someone were to find out they were in the same place at the same time it would mean very bad things for Chase.

Chase didn't deserve this. He didn't deserve to be painted as the bad guy. After what he had told me tonight I knew that Brett's disappearance had hurt him far more then he was ever going to admit. I could even sense the hurt and betrayal he felt when mentioning the reasons behind the destruction of their friendship. I could tell just from the way he talked about Brett's father that he hated the man, there was an underlying anger that ran deep below the surface.

I wish there was a way to help Brett. He was obviously running from his family, but why haven't the police and my father even considered this? Nobody but Chase seems to have come to this conclusion. Brett had told

Chase himself that he couldn't go back. But he wanted to fix things, wanted to make things right.

Never have I ever felt so helpless. I close my eyes as sleep slowly drags me under.

My alarm clock screams at me, demanding me to get up. I wasn't even sure of how many hours sleep I had got last night but I knew it was few.

"What the fuck? It's only 7 am!" A tired Chase groans from the floor giving me the biggest fright.

"Holy shit! I forgot you were here," I say peering over the side of my bed. Chase's hair is as messy as usual, his green eyes now focusing on me. I feel my cheeks heat up as I feel his eyes run along my face. I take the time to analyse his bruise. It doesn't look good but definitely better than last night.

"Really? That's surprising considering the number of times I heard you mumble my name in your sleep," Chase chuckles, teasing me.

He sits himself up and I can't help but let my eyes wander over his bare chest. How is it even possible to have a body that perfectly sculptured?

"Having fun there?" he asks. I raise my gaze to meet his smirk. Cocky bastard.

"Don't flatter yourself, Chase, I was looking at your injury," I say meeting his smirk. It wasn't a complete lie. Yes, I had been looking at his bare chest but that's where his injury was. I look at it again and just looking at it makes me wince.

I get out of my bed before he can make another one of his egotistical comments and head to my wardrobe getting out my school dress. I feel Chase's green eyes watching my every move. Without even turning back to look at him I make my way to my bathroom and close the door.

As much as I would prefer not to go to school if my dad ever found out I had skipped I would be in deep trouble.

I finish getting ready and make my way back to my bedroom. Chase has not moved from his position, his gaze fixated on something in my wardrobe. He turns his head to me as I walk into the room.

"Is that your dress for the dance?" He asks, his voice low and husky, eyes watching me closely before turning back to the red dress I bought the other week.

"Yeah," is all I say in response. He nods his head slightly, giving me a look up and down as if he is imagining in the dress. I feel my cheeks blush as I just stand in the doorway unsure of what to do.

"Why don't you want to go?" I ask him, deep down hoping he's had a change in heart.

"Dances aren't really my thing. School events, in general, aren't really my thing," he shrugs.

"So," I say, "What is your thing?" I ask. I can't believe the question even exits my mouth.

I feel his eyes latch onto mine as if there is a string tying us together, not one of us daring to make a move. I watch as a million emotions pour over his face all at once before he quickly covers it up again.

"I really don't know anymore," he says breaking eye contact, his gaze adverting to the floor.

My eyes focus on his lips, only hours ago were they on mine. How I crave that feeling now. The feeling of his hand on my face. The lack of space between us.

I manage to break myself out of my trance, "Come have some breakfast when you're ready."

I walk down the corridor to the kitchen where I grab out some cereal and milk. I take my bowl and go sit at the table. A few minutes later I hear Chase's footsteps padding down the hallway as he winces with each step. He has thankfully put a shirt on, the one he came in last night.

"I need to get home before mum wakes up, so she doesn't see, you know, my face," he says, leaning against the kitchen bench.

"Are you alright driving home?" I ask, hoping he'll say no so I could spend more time with him.

"Yeah I'm fine," He nods. "I was able to drive here in the middle of the night so should be able to drive the short ride home."

For a moment we just stare at each other, both of us wanting to ask the same question but both too scared to do so. What happens next? What happens after that kiss?

I stand up as he starts walking to the door.

"See you in biology?" I ask as he opens the door. I silently curse myself as the words leave my mouth sounding more like a plea than a question.

He turns around giving me a small smirk, "See you in biology."

I watch as he turns around and starts walking down the street towards his car. Thank god he parked further down or my dad would have noticed his presence last night.

He suddenly stops and quickly turns around, "Hey Sage, thank you for last night." As the words leave his mouth he turns around again.

I can't wipe the idiotic grin present on my face as I go back inside and finish my breakfast.

~~~~~~~~~~~~~~~~~~~~~~~~~~~~~~~~

☆ Please vote and comment ☆
~~~~~~~~~~~~~~~~~~~~~~~~~~~~~~~~

Chapter 26 ~ Chase

Chase's POV

I can't handle this right now.

She is all my mind is thinking about, it keeps drifting unknowingly back to a certain brunette and it is driving me absolutely fucking insane, I can't get her out of my head no matter how hard I try.

I squeeze my eyes shut in hopes that it will miraculously wipe Sage from my mind, but nothing seems to be working. I need to clear my head of Sage and fast.

She is messing with my brain more than she realises, and I have no clue what to do.

Shit.

I unknowingly squeeze the wheel of my car tighter as I drive from school to the warehouse, earlier I had received an angry phone call from Aaron demanding I go see him as soon as possible.

I pull up and park in the nearest spot available as I see the faint outline of a figure standing about 100 metres away, only Aaron is crazy enough to wait out in the rain for someone.

He notices my car and begins to make his way over to me. I roll out my shoulders hoping to release some of my built-up tension, but nothing seems to work.

"Chase," Aaron says as he strolls over to me. He is careful in the way he positions himself, far enough away to escape if needs to, but close enough to be heard.

"Yes?" I ask the last thing I want is to stand here, cold in a car park. I am much more leaning towards a warm shower currently after my last 24 hours and a long ass nap.

"I want you to go pro," He states, I frown in return to that statement.

"I've lost some of my best fighters and I need to show you off," he continues.

"Think of it as more money," He says, hoping that I'll jump at this opportunity as if he is some miracle worker giving me a second chance at life. Except, I don't want it.

I never have.

Once you go pro there is no going back, and I never want to end up so tightly wound up in the webs of fighting that I can't escape.

"No," I state.

"It isn't a question, more a statement," he growls back, voicing his distaste for me turning down his offer.

"I said no," I repeat. I'm not going to change my mind, no money in the world is worth selling yourself up to become someone's puppet.

Aaron already has enough control over my life as it is.

There is no way in hell I am letting him have any more say in my life than what he already has.

He is shit out of luck.

"Chase, you will regret this," he says, anger in his tone.

"We'll see about that," I counter.

"If you don't go pro, you're done. The first fight is Saturday, you show or you're out," He replies as if that will make me cave. He doesn't know me. He should know that. I. Am. Not. Weak.

"Bye Aaron," I state nonchalantly, but as I turn to leave, he calls out my name one last time.

"Chase, I will see you there Saturday. You will make the right decision because you don't want to find out what will happen if you don't," he threatens.

"And if you actually don't show, I will ruin you." He says, his tone holding a sense of finality that I don't like, his snake-like eyes piercing through my own. His face has a sinister smirk on it.

Going pro meant no school. It meant full time-fighting. Full-time training.

I had sworn that I was never going to let fighting become my life before I had come back.

I am not going to give up school, it is the only way I can escape this shitty town. It is my only hope at freedom, and I am not about to let it slip through my hands like sand because Aaron says I should be afraid of the consequences. I don't take to people threatening me kindly.

I have nothing left to say, so with that, I turn and make my way back to the car.

Everyone suddenly thinks they have some sort of control over my life, I am not used to so many people meddling in my business trying to make it their own.

I am not a fan of people becoming involved in my decisions. Never have been.

I will figure this out on my own like I usually do.

My mind is tired and fuzzy. There is an ache forming at the back of my head that is beginning to become as regular as my heart beating. My brain hurts from all this thinking, all these unanswered questions.

Where is Brett? Was he lying when he said he was coming back? Was he truly going to be able to fix this mess? What did Aaron possibly have on me that could ruin me? My head is spinning, thumping against my skull, making me massage my temples to find some sort of release, that is never coming.

This is a never-ending vicious cycle. Playing on repeat.

And currently, there is only one voice that I want to hear.

"Chase?" She asks through the phone, her voice wrapping around my throat making it hard to breathe. How did she have so much control over my body?

What is she doing to me? Just hearing her voice is making my head spin.

"Chase?" Her voice is more urgent now, growing in alarm.

"Hey," I say, waiting as silence follows.

"What are you doing? Why are you calling?" she asks.

"Honestly I just need to hear your voice right now," I say. I am drained and tired, but hearing her voice makes the pain in my head lessen. She is becoming a drug to me, and there is no denying I am becoming more and more addicted by every passing day.

"Ummm..." She trails off. "Chase is everything ok? What happened?" She's worried.

"Don't worry sweetheart, it's nothing I can't handle," I reply, not wanting to dump my problems on her. I continue, "Just talk," I say trying to distract her.

"About what?" She asks back. I can practically feel how eager she is to know why I called her, but I didn't have a logical answer to give her.

"Anything," I say.

I want to know what she is thinking, anything to distract me from the timeline that has now been placed on me. Between now and Friday I need to decide. Am I turning my back on fighting? But if I don't go through with it what does Aaron have in store for me?

"Give me a thought for a thought," she replies. Sage is fishing for information on what happened before I called her, she knows somethings up. You can't keep anything from that girl.

"Chase," she is going to ask what happened. I know she is. I cut her off before she can continue.

"You know what is tearing me up inside?" I ask.

"What?" she asks, full of curiosity.

"The feeling that I need to go to this dance Saturday, to see you in that dress of yours," I reply, listening as she takes in a sharp breath in reply. I decide to continue because I have never been a fan of silence. "And I also don't know why I'm telling you this, or why I felt the need to call you but here I am" I finish.

The silence that follows is deafening.

"That's two thoughts," she says, her voice floating lightly through the phone.

"Well, I guess you owe me two in return then don't you sweetheart," I say smirking into the phone.

"Ok my first thought is that I think you should definitely consider going to the dance, and my second thought is that I am wondering how you will look in a tux," she says.

And those words make my heart stall in my chest.

"Is that so Sage Hill?" I ask and listen as she laughs in response.

~~~~~~~~~~~~~~~~~~~~~~~~~~~~~~~

☆ Please vote and comment ☆
~~~~~~~~~~~~~~~~~~~~~~~~~~~~~~~

Chapter 27 ~ Sage

S age's POV

My eyes grow wide as I take in the room in front of me. Our school gym has been transformed into a room full of balloons and streamers. Tables line the walls as students hover around the food and punch.

I look at May who is just as wide-eyed as me. She is wearing a spaghetti strapped, navy blue dress with a slit up the side. Her heels, like mine, are silver. Her brunette hair is tied up into a flawless messy bun, accentuating her hazel eyes.

She smiles at me and gives my shoulder a squeeze, "Ready?" she asks.

"Ready," I say, giving her a smile as we walk into the gym.

I am wearing the red dress and silver heels I bought the day I saw Brett. I have tied my hair up into a classy ponytail.

We immediately notice Sarah and Alice standing with their dates at a nearby table. May and I quickly make our way over, desperate to see our friends.

Sarah is wearing a strapless black dress with her long brown hair out. Alice, on the other hand, is wearing a baby pink dress with a halter neck and white heels. Her blonde hair is tied back into a gorgeous messy braid.

"You both look stunning!" Sarah smiles at May and I as we all embrace in a group hug.

"So do you guys," I say.

I say hello to Sarah's date Liam and Alice's date Mason.

Liam had asked Sarah to go to the dance with him as soon as the dance had been announced. They were so obviously a thing but neither of them would openly admit their true feelings for one another.

Mason and Alice on the other- hand have been dating for over a year. They absolutely adore each other.

Thank god May is single or else I'd be a loner at this dance.

I can't help but look around the room, hoping to find a pair of intense green eyes staring back at me. But I have no idea whether Chase has decided to come or not.

The butterflies that rose in my chest the other night when he told me he was considering coming to the dance so he could see me in my dress have failed to vanish since. We ended up talking for hours about the most pointless of things but there was not a second in which I wasn't smiling.

"Is he here?" May asks eagerly, noticing I had zoned out.

I had told May the brief details about Chase and I's confusing relationship, obviously leaving out anything to do with Brett and Chase's fighting. She didn't even seem fazed that he was a suspect in a disappearance case but why am I surprised? May is the biggest hopeless romantic you will ever meet.

"Can't see him," I say, unable to hide the disappointment from my voice.

I have no idea what Chase and I are. The situation at hand is too difficult to even give us a label, that's if he even wants one. We are always flirting and after that kiss, I can't help but want to always be around him. Maybe once this case is over and Chase is in the clear something will happen. But I don't know how long that will take and I don't think I can wait much longer. My head is such a mess but when I'm with him it feels clear.

"I'm sure he will turn up," she says giving me a reassuring smile. "Knowing him he probably just wants to make an entrance." I can't help but laugh at that statement. No matter what time Chase rocks up he will be automatically making a scene.

I was honestly so terrified at the prospect of having to come to Mapleville, having to start life all over again. But it hasn't been what I thought it would be. I have made friends. Bloody good friends.

I look at May. I have never had a best friend but she was certainly coming to close to it.

"Come on, let's go dance," she laughs as she drags me onto the dance floor.

We find ourselves in the middle of the crowd, surrounded by people who I didn't even realise attended our school. The endless amount of bodies created a claustrophobic environment but we were too busy dancing our hearts out to care.

Song after song goes by until May and I turn to each other both out of breath.

"Punch?" I ask.

"Yes please," she says. We find our way out of the crowd of people and make our way over to the nearby tables.

I look at the time on my phone. It is 8:30 pm. We have been here for an hour. I find myself scanning the crowd again but don't find the messy haired Chase anywhere.

"Let's go sit," May says, making her way over to our table. I spy Mason, Alice, Sarah and Liam on the dancefloor.

I sit down and take a long sip from my cup. The fruit flavoured punch slides down my throat, cooling me down amidst the stuffiness in the room.

"Hello Ladies," A deep voice says from behind me, causing May and I both to jump in fright. Two guys walk around to the other side of our table before sitting in Alice and Mason's seats.

"My name is Kyle and this is Conner," a guy with dirty blonde hair and dark brown eyes says pointing at his friend Conner who is blonde with hazel eyes. An arrogant smile is plastered on both of their faces.

"We couldn't help but noticing you girls were all alone and we were wondering if you wanted to come and hang out with us," Conner says, a cheeky glint present in his eyes.

"I don't think we've met I'm May and this is Sage," May says, giving them a wary look.

Recognition passes over their faces as they exchange a glance before focusing their eyes on me.

"Sage? As in the girl that hangs out with Chase Rivers?" Kyle asks with wide eyes.

I exchange a look with May, unaware of what to say. The boys ignore my silence, pressing for more information.

"Huh, interesting," Conner says, leaning towards us intrigued, I can already tell he's the confident one out of the two. "So how does it feel to hang out with the most dangerous guy in school?" He asks.

"You don't know him," I say defensively. Nobody knew him. Everybody saw him as a cruel, dangerous guy when he was really so far from that, or at least he is when he has been with me lately.

"So, where is your boyfriend tonight?" Kyle asks, seeming to find the situation quite amusing.

"Maybe out murdering someone?" Conner says smirking as they both erupt into laughter.

I am seeing red. How dare they? How fucking dare they?

"Get lost," I say, anger evident in my tone.

"Aw is somebody sad their boyfriend didn't turn up?" Kyle smiles.

However, his grin falters as he looks behind me. In fact, his skin begins to pale as worry fills he and Conner's face.

"What are you talking about? I'm right here," A voice snarls at Conner and Kyle. "Now if you guys are done being douchebags you can leave these ladies alone."

I turn around to find Chase standing behind my chair eyes focused on the two boys sitting across from May and I.

His hair is slightly neater than usual, his bruise on his face still evident but fading. My mouth feels dry as I take in the whole of him. Chase in a suit is definitely an image I want to remember forever.

I lift my eyes to meet his which are now focused solely on me. His signature smirk plastered on his face.

"Why do you look so surprised to see me, sweetheart?" He says with a wink, that makes my heart begin to flutter frantically.

~~~~~~~~~~~~~~~~~~~~~~~~~~~~~~~~~~

☆ Please vote and comment ☆
~~~~~~~~~~~~~~~~~~~~~~~~~~~~~~~~~~

Chapter 28 ~ Chase

C hase's POV

~ 2 hours earlier ~

I have no idea what to do. My mind is literally split in two, it feels like someone is gripping each side ofmy head and trying to tear it down the middle. Half of me wants to show up at the dance and put the nagging thoughts of what Sage would look like in that dress to rest, but the other half doesn't want to discover what Aaron would retaliate with if I don't show up at his fight.

Earlier mum had come into my room, lightly clutching a suit in her hand telling me she had heard about the dance a week earlier and had gotten me a suit, thinking that I might change my mind at the last minute. The hope in her eyes made me want to drop my worries about Aaron and just go to the dance.

Dancing isn't my thing, but I can't stop the nagging feeling within me that wants to see Sage.

Something deep down churns when I think of Sage dancing with someone else. The thought undoubtedly makes me uncomfortable.

I can't stomach it.

And with that thought, I decide that whatever Aaron has planned doesn't matter. I am worrying about giving him control over my life if I am to go pro, but I am also letting him play me along by worrying about what he has over me. Besides, there is no denying that if I am to play by his rules, that he may pull this card again when it suits him in the future. I can't let that happen.

I stand from my bed and glance at the suit that is neatly laid out on my bed from earlier, where it has stayed untouched for the past few hours as I stewed on what to do. I grab it and make my way towards the shower to get ready.

Glancing at the time I realise that the dance had already started a little over 20 minutes ago. I am not someone to show up early anyway. I shower and get dressed in the suit. I make my way downstairs to where my mum is seated curled up on the couch watching the tv with interest.

"Hey mum, I'll be back later tonight. Don't wait up," I say as I kiss her cheek before turning towards the door. I can tell that she is happy I am going by the way her eyes light up a little as she glances at me.

"Chase," she says catching my attention, her light green vivid eyes catching mine.

"You look great," She states getting up and giving me a light hug.

"Thanks, bye mum," I reply, before walking out the door and towards my car.

I drive towards the school and park my car before walking my way towards the gym and entering. My eyes scan the crowd, taking in the faces of people who are huddled in groups, scattered across the room. I notice Caleb in the corner of the gym leant up against the wall with a glass in one hand, his grey hard assessing eyes flash to mine as if he can sense my eyes on him. He nods his head at me, before turning his attention to something else.

It doesn't take long for my eyes find the certain brunette I came here for. I notice that she sits at a table with one other girl who I have seen with her before and two guys. I frown as I look around the circle and focus my attention onto Sage, her shoulders are tense, and her hands are scrunched into fists at her sides.

What the fuck is happening over there?

I make my way to the table and get close enough to hear a snippet of the conversation.

"So where is your boyfriend tonight?" the idiot I think is named Kyle asks, addressing Sage. But before she can answer the other one buts in beating her too it.

"Maybe out murdering someone?" Conner taunts, as a smirk flashes across his face. That son of a bitch.

"Get lost," Sage replies, venom dripping off her words.

"Aw is somebody sad their boyfriend didn't turn up?" Kyle asks mockingly.

This is my cue to intervene.

"What are you talking about? I'm right here" I address them both, watching as their arrogant grins they were sporting seconds earlier are completely wiped off their faces. "Now if you guys are done being douchebags you can leave these ladies alone," I state.

I look down at Sage and watch as she looks me up and down, before blushing slightly and meeting my gaze. I smirk in reply.

"Why do you look so surprised to see me sweetheart?" I tease looking down at her.

Before anything more can be said I look up at the two boys.

"I suggest you two get lost right about now," I state looking as they both get up to leave. Good.

"You actually came," she says, not hiding the surprise in her voice.

"Well as I told you I had to see what you look like in that dress," I reply, but before she can reply I continue, "And let me tell you, you didn't disappoint," I finish.

"You don't scrub up too bad yourself," She says her bright blue azure eyes meeting mine.

I turn my attention to the girl next to her.

"Do you mind if I steal Sage away for a minute?" I ask.

"Uh no, she's all yours. I need to go find Alice anyways..." she trails off but not before sending Sage a small wink, which doesn't go unnoticed by me.

"Let's dance," I say taking Sage's hand in mine and leading her to the dance floor.

Once we arrive I turn to face her. Sage looks up at me and offers me a small smile. Before she can possibly overthink this more than she already is, I grab her hips and pull her closer to me. She remains still as her eyes flash to mine.

"This is the time that you're meant to put your hands around my neck sweetheart," I say, and wait as she shakes her head lightly letting out a small laugh before she does as I said.

She places her head gently against my shoulder, and I worry that she may hear the fact that my heartbeat has slightly sped up from having her this close to me.

"What changed your mind into coming?" she mumbles into my chest as we slowly sway to the music.

"I think we both know the reason I showed tonight," I say lightly, leaning my head on top of hers, and let her soft scent of roses engulf me, making me let out a sigh of content. I could happily stay like this all night.

She looks up at me from under her lashes, and my heart stalls slightly in my chest.

I need some fresh air or I am going to kiss her again, in front of the whole school this time.

"Would you like to go outside for some fresh air?" I ask looking down at her.

"Yeah sure, just let me grab my purse," she replies before turning, and before I can protest she slips out of my arms and makes her way back the table that she was previously seated at.

I make my way towards the door meeting her there. She looks up at me once she arrives.

"Let's go," she says, before turning and making her way outside, slipping her hand in mine and pulling me along with her.

But before we are able to make it to the end of the steps I notice something that replaces the small smile on my face with a frown.

What are Sage's dad and a police officer doing here at the school dance?

Sage looks back at me in confusion wondering why I have stopped in my tracks and then follows my eyes to where her dad and another man in uniform are making their way towards us.

"Dad?" Sage asks confusion clear in her question.

"Not now Sage. Go inside," her dad commands before his eyes turn to me, not before noticing our intertwined hands, causing a disapproving scowl to appear on his face.

"Chase you need to come with us immediately. We have received new evidence in Brett's case and we need you down at the police station now," The police officer says addressing me sternly.

"What are you talking about? You've already searched my house and found nothing. What have you suddenly found that would change anything at this point?" I ask confused. I feel Sage's hand tighten around mine.

"We have reason to believe you have been lying about not knowing the whereabouts of Brett throughout his disappearance," he states meeting my cold glare.

What the fuck?

Before I am able to respond he holds up his phone showing a photo.

A photo that makes my heart stop beating.

A photo that makes it feel like someone has grabbed my throat and squeezed the air out of my lungs making it hard to breathe.

A photo that makes me look completely and utterly guilty.

Shit.

~~~~~~~~~~~~~~~~~~~~~~~~~~~~~~~~~~~
~~~~~~~~~~~~~~~~~~~~~~~~~~~~~~~~~~~

☆ Please vote and comment ☆

Chapter 29 ~ Sage

S age's POV

I look back at Chase, confused at to why he has suddenly stopped. He's looking past me, a frown etched on his face. I follow his gaze and almost choke when I see my dad and Officer Dylan walking towards the school gym.

Why the hell is my dad at my school dance?

"Dad?" I ask, not hiding the confusion from my tone.

"Not now Sage. Go inside," he demands. Well, that is like a slap to the face.

His gaze drifts to Chase and I's hands which are still intertwined. Not even the stern look he gives us could cause me to drop Chase's hand.

"Chase you need to come with us immediately. We have received new evidence in Brett's case and we need you down at the police station now," Officer Dylan says, his eyes focused on Chase waiting as if he thinks Chase is going to make a run for it.

New evidence? Why does new evidence have anything to do with Chase? Why does he need to go immediately? What did they find that has caused them to feel the need to come to a school dance to take him away?

"What are you talking about? You've already searched my house and found nothing. What have you suddenly found that would change anything at this point?" Chase asks confused.

I tighten my grip on his hand to let him know I'm with him. I'm on his side.

"We have reason to believe you have been lying about not knowing the whereabouts of Brett throughout his disappearance," Officer Dylan says coldly.

Oh shit.

He reaches into his pocket, extracting his phone. He holds it out to Chase and I. The image on the screen makes my head pound.

The photo is of Chase and Brett. It must have been from the other night when Brett showed up at Chase's fight. The picture shows them talking, neither looking pleased Chase in particular. Before I can analyse it further he whips the phone away from view.

I suck in a deep breath and step closer to Chase. This can't be happening. This time his hand tightens around mine, implying he doesn't want to let go. As if he Is afraid of what will happen if he does.

"Sage, go back into the gym," my dad says giving me a serious look.

"No," I say, standing my ground, showing who's side I am choosing.

How am I supposed to go back into the gym and enjoy my night when the guy I like is being taken in for interrogation for the one-hundredth time?

Not to mention that I am just as guilty for the thing he is going to be interrogated about.

"Excuse me?" He asks in a tone of voice I've rarely heard from him.

"I'm coming," I say, looking at him directly in the eyes.

"Sage, what the fuck are you doing?" Chase hisses into my ear, quietly enough that I know my dad and Dylan wouldn't be able to make out what he is saying.

I turn and look into his green eyes and analyse the look of complete and utter shock on his face.

"I'm just as guilty as you," I whisper. "I saw him too. I saw him first."

"No, I won't let you take the fall for me," He whispers, his eyes urgent.

"Well, I won't let you take the fall for something that involves both of us," I whisper and turn back to my father and Officer Dylan who looks gobsmacked.

"Sage, I will not ask again. Go back into that gym right now," My father says, eyes blazing.

"No, I am coming," I say sternly. I hear Chase curse behind me.

"This is an investigation, Sage. We have no reason to investigate you," Officer Dylan says impatiently.

"Yes, you do," I say watching as both of their faces turn from anger to confusion.

"Sage, don't do this," Chase pleads, squeezing my hand.

But I have to. There's no way I can let Chase go while I just walk away as if I am innocent. I don't think I could live with myself, live with the guilt.

My dad will be mad. Not just mad but furious. I have kept this from him for so long.

"What are you talking about Sage? This isn't a time for jokes," My dad says seriously.

"I'm not joking. Chase isn't the only one who has seen Brett. I have too," I say, putting as much confidence into my voice as possible.

"Are you trying to tell me that you were here when this photo was taken?" Officer Dylan asks confused.

"No, but I saw him a few weeks ago when I went to go buy this dress," I say looking down at my red dress.

"Look, Sage, if you are trying to save Chase's ass I suggest you stop now," My dad warns.

Shock hits me like a wave. He really didn't believe me.

"I'm telling the truth. I saw him," I say emphasising the word saw.

I watch as hurt washes over my father's face. I have kept something so valuable from him. Something that affects his job. I made a choice. I chose Chase over my dad when I hardly even knew the boy who is now gripping my hand tightly as if trying to protect me from the wrath I am about to endure.

"Did you know about this?" Officer Dylan demands, looking at Chase accusingly.

"Yes," Chase says, running his free hand through his hair pulling on the ends as if he is trying to wake himself from a nightmare. "Just let her go. She has nothing to do with this. I'll answer all your questions."

I feel him rub his thumb over my hand in three circular motions.

"I'm sorry but you both have to come to the police station. Immediately. We've already wasted enough time as it is," Officer Dylan interjects while giving my father a sympathetic look.

I lower my eyes to the ground, unable to meet my father's broken eyes. I feel Chase tug on my hand as he leads me to the police car parked near where we are standing. We walk past my dad and Dylan, Chase's grip tightening on my hand if that is even possible.

He opens the door of the car for me. I gather my dress and hop in, a million thoughts running through my mind at once.

If I had left Chase to take the fall all on his own I would have never forgiven myself. It would eat up at me forever until I eventually told my father what I knew. Either way, I would lose. I chose the way of honesty. However, honesty is what is going to ruin my father's trust in me.

I slide across, making room for Chase who quickly gets in and closes the door.

"Sage, what the hell are you doing?" He says, his eyes wide as he looks at me perplexed.

"The same thing you'd do for me," I say, my voice coming out a lot stronger than I feel.

His expression softens as he just analyses me. I can hear the footsteps of Officer Dylan and my father approaching.

"I came here tonight to see you. Not to see you be dragged into this hell ride with me," Chase says, his voice low as he takes my hand in his.

"Well I wasn't about to stand back and watch as the boy I like is taken away in a police car," I whisper loud enough for him to hear as Dylan and my dad get in the car.

Chapter 30 ~ Chase

C hase's POV

"Well I wasn't about to stand back and watch as the boy I like is taken away in a police car," She says, just loud enough for me to hear.

Boy she likes?

My mind is spinning, as if someone has taken my head and is shaking it around like a snow globe, muddling my thoughts up and leaving them to drift around and land all over the place, leaving me utterly confused and scrambling to pick them up and put them in order. Before I am able to even process a response to Sage's dad and the police officer enter the car.

Them being this close in proximity to Sage and I creates a strong feeling of complete and utter tension. I roll my neck from side to side hoping to lift this imaginary weight that feels like it is crushing me.

There is one thing I am certain of, and that is that I cannot let Sage take the fall for me.

I can't and won't let her.

I turn my eyes to meet Sage's dad's in the rear-view mirror and there is no mistaking the pent-up anger that can be felt rolling off him in waves. He is beyond mad. He has just found out his daughter betrayed him and kept a massive thing from him. I don't know whether he's disappointed in his daughter or fuming at me for involving Sage in my problems. Or maybe both.

I can't contain the small smile that slips onto my face, she chose me.

She chose me over everyone else, and something within me shifts.

I feel a small spark of happiness.

We pull into the police station and I notice that Sage slightly shifts in her seat. She's nervous I can tell by the way she begins to fiddle with her hands. Sage's dad and Dylan leave the car and I lean over and tilt my head towards her.

"Calm down, it's going to be okay," I whisper, noticing that she slightly relaxes.

"Let's get this over with," she says glancing at me, giving me a small smile before she turns and gets out of the car, and I follow close behind.

We make our way up the steps, following close behind Sage's dad and the police officer. Sage's dad glances over his shoulder to check that we are still following as if he's worried that we will turn away and make a run for it.

"Sit here, and we will be back in a minute," The officer says before turning and making his way around a corner with Sage's dad following close behind.

"Sage," I say catching her diverted attention.

"Yeah?" she asks, her voice light and airy.

"Thanks for before," I mutter not sure what to say. "And about what you said in the car..." I begin but get interrupted by the same officer from before walking around the corner.

"Sage, you need to come with me," He says, and I watch as Sage's eyes flicker to me, clearly reluctant to leave.

"I'll be back in a second," she says before following the officer out of the room.

I watch her go, her red dress flowing after her. I'm still stunned that she defied her father in order to prove a point on which side she was on.

Mine.

And that was one of the best things I heard in a long time.

I sit and let my eyes flitter around the room, the beige colour makes me begin to feel nauseous and uneasy. I look at the clock wishing for the time to speed up and for Sage to be out of the interrogation room. She doesn't belong in there.

Before I can think about what's happening in the room the sound of yelling begins to filter down the hallway. But that isn't what catches my attention. What makes my head turn so quickly I think I may get whiplash is the voice of who's yelling.

Sage, she is yelling something at whoever is in the room with her which I can only presume is her father.

It doesn't take long before the voices grow louder, followed closely by the sound of footsteps until they turn the corner and are standing right in front of me.

"Dad you're not listening, Chase isn't guilty, but you don't believe me do you? You've already made your mind up haven't you? This whole town has, just because he was the last one who was possibly seen with him means that he is guilty?"

"He lied Sage, he said he didn't know where Brett was, but he did!" Her father replies, struggling to keep his voice from raising.

"So did I!" she hisses back

"Sage, you are going to leave, go home and we will continue this discussion when I am finished here," Her father says looking down at her sternly, his eyes silently pleading with her to agree. "For once just do as your told."

Too bad for him my girl isn't one to listen to anyone.

Once she has her mind set on something, there is no undoing it.

Did I just say my girl?

"Go home? You want me to go home? That house isn't a home, it's four walls and a roof. But you're never even home long enough to realise that there is nothing homely about that place, are you? Because you're always working too late or you are too busy. Ever since mum's death you've spent your time drowning yourself in your work to distract yourself from the fact that she isn't here that you forgot about me in the process," She says her voice broken, her confident demeanour fading slightly as a single tear runs down her cheek.

My chest begins to tighten and ache.

I turn my attention to her dad, who looks as if he has been suddenly been punched in the stomach.

Sage turns and walks over to me. She looks up at me, I focus my eyes on hers and let them flicker down to the tear that has escaped. Before I can think I reach my hand up and cup her cheek and let my thumb rub lightly along her skin capturing the tear before it can fall any further.

"Hey, hey," I say making her eyes find mine once again. "It's ok, we're going to figure this out, no matter what," I say a silent promise beneath my words, glancing down letting my eyes look from her eyes down to her lips for a second.

After this is over I am going to kiss those sweet lips of hers.

"It's ok go find your friend. Stay at her house for the night, don't spend it alone after what has happened," I say rubbing my hand over her cheek again trying to get her to calm down.

I can practically feel the frown coming from her dad as he assesses the exchange between the two of us. But right now I couldn't give a shit.

"You're fine sweetheart, and so am I," I lean my head down against hers and lightly press my lips to her forehead, savouring the moment, because God knows her dad isn't going to let me this close to her ever again after tonight.

She looks up and nods at me meekly, before turning and leaving without even glancing at her father.

"Sage I've organised a lift, it's waiting out front," her dad says before she manages to make it to the door.

"No," she says pivoting around to look at her father, "I can figure out a lift myself," she fires back.

"Sage," I say strolling over to her before she is able to leave. "Take this, it has a phone number on it, call it and say that I gave it to you and that you need a lift. His name is Caleb and he'll help you," I say low enough for only her and I to be able to hear.

Her eyes travel up and meet mine before she nods and turns and disappears through the doors.

If looks could kill I would have been dead minutes ago with the look Sage's dad is sending my way currently.

"That is you, you started this! You're the reason she's wrapped up in all this," Her dad says anger evident in his tone.

"No," I state back "This is all you, don't get mad with me because I was there for your daughter when you weren't," I retort.

And with that, I turn and walk past him into the interrogation room.

Chapter 31 ~ Sage

Sage's POV

I take one last look at Chase, taking in all of him out of fear that my father is unlikely to let me within 10 meters of him ever again.

I resist the urge to lean up and kiss him, but I decide against it knowing that it will only make matters worse.

I turn and walk through the police station doors, my red dress flowing after me. This isn't how I thought this night would end. I thought I'd go to the dance, have fun with my friends and hopefully see Chase. While all those things had happened so did the part where I ended up going to the police station for interrogation.

After Officer Dylan had told me to explain what had happened the day I saw Brett, my dad came into the room.

I know he is hurt and he has every right to be, but so am I. I have spent the last few years of my life with what feels like no family members. It was hard enough losing my mum but to lose my dad too even when he's not literally gone tears me up a little inside.

Because of that, I lost it at him in the middle of the police station, in front of my dad, in front of Chase and any other nearby officer. But I don't fucking care.

I squeeze my eyes shut as another tear escapes my eye, rolling down my cheek. I quickly wipe it away. I wish I was back at the dance. Back on the dancefloor with Chase's arms around my waist as I placed my head on his chest. I felt as if I could stay there forever, breathing in his musky aroma as he held me to him.

I look around the dark carpark and quickly take out my phone. The screen lights up, text message after text message from May. Shit. I am meant to be staying at her house tonight. I look at the time displayed on my phone. 1 am. The dance is well and truly over.

I look at the piece of paper in my hands with a number on it that Chase gave me as I left. I dial the number and it rings three times before someone picks up.

"Hello?" a deep voice says from the other end of the phone. "Who is this?" He questions.

"Sage," I say, wondering who this Caleb kid is.

"Sage? As in the famous Sage Hill who has Chase whipped?" He asks feigning fake surprise. I can almost sense the smirk he is wearing through the phone.

I don't know what to say. Ignoring his comment, I ask, "Is this Caleb?"

"Yeah, I'm Caleb. Why do you ask?" He questions curiously.

"Chase gave me your number. I need your help," I say.

"Look, I really only find information for people during the daytime so maybe you could ring back in the morning?" He asks, stifling a yawn.

"I don't need information," I say. "I need you to come pick me up. Chase said you'd help."

"Why can't lover boy pick you up?" He teases.

"We are both kind of stuck at the police station right now and he said if I called you, that you would be able to give me a lift to my friend's house," I say pleadingly.

"The police station? What are you guys Bonnie and Clyde now?" He says with a slight chuckle.

"Please Caleb," I say, not in the mood for jokes.

"Yeah ok, I guess. I'll be there in 5 minutes," he says and with that, he hangs up.

Well, at least I have a lift. Now I need a place to stay. I read through all my messages from May.

Hey Sage where r u?

R u with Chase?

Did you guys leave?

Sageeeeeee

R u still coming back to my house?

Sage, I am about to be picked up where r u?

Sage pls respond

I'm in the car my brother is so annoying and wouldn't even wait 5 minutes for u

I hope you're ok

Pls respond

I quickly call her. She picks up on the first ring.

"Sage, what the hell? Where did you go?" She asks, voice full of concern.

"Look it's a long story. Is it alright if I get dropped at your house?" I ask, hoping the answer will be yes. There is no way I want to go stay at my house and have to deal with the wrath of my father.

"Yeah of course just text me when you get here," she says.

"Thank you so much! You're the best," I say and hang up as I see a car pull into the parking lot. The dark car comes to a stop in front of me.

The front window rolls down, revealing a boy my age wearing a beanie over his dark hair, trying to tame the messy locks. His grey eyes analyse me, noticing I'm still in my formal dress and heels. Hopefully, my makeup is still intact and my mascara hasn't run.

"I'm Caleb," he says giving me a slight nod of his head.

"Sage," is all I say as I make my way around to the other side of the car and hop in.

"So where am I taking you?" he asks.

I give him May's address and he gives a slight nod.

"Just so you know I don't own a taxi service. I'm only doing this because Chase asked for it and you're his girl," he says, not taking his eyes off the road.

His girl. Am I Chase's girl?

"Got it," I say, deciding to let his comment slide.

"Rough night?" he asks giving me a quick glance.

"You could say that," I mumble. Desperate to change the topic I ask, "So how did you and Chase become friends?"

"I guess you could say we both don't quite belong. Somewhat outsiders in society, so we came to sometimes depend on each other when needed, he says, his grey eyes lacking emotion. "Is Chase still at the police station?" He asks, changing the topic back, deflecting it from himself.

"Yeah," I say. I hadn't wanted to leave him there but he had urged me to go. Besides, I couldn't bear to be in the same building as my father.

"Don't worry I'm not going to pry for details. I'm not like that," he says giving me a small smile.

I can see why Caleb and Chase are friends. They don't care about the gossip. They'd much rather live in isolation.

The rest of the car ride is silent. Silent but not awkward.

He pulls up at May's house.

"Thank you, Caleb," I say giving him a small smile.

"All good. Tell Chase to call me when he's out," He says glancing over at me and giving me a small smile. I nod and get out of the car. I text May and the front door to her house opens almost immediately.

"Oh my gosh, Sage. Are you alright?" She asks, her brunette hair tied up in a messy ponytail. She has changed out of her dress and is wearing track pants and an oversized T-shirt.

"Yeah I'm fine just tired," I say as she opens the door wider and lets me in.

She shows me to her room, leading me along a corridor with numerous doors neatly lining the walls. Since when did May have so many siblings? We reach her room and she lends me some clothes to wear.

May can tell I'm not ready to talk and thankfully doesn't push me for answers.

My eyes feel heavy and all I want to do is cry but I push the tears back. I think of Chase. I wonder if he is still at the police station. Surely he will text me when he comes out.

It isn't fair. I am just as guilty as him yet he is the one who is going to be punished. I think of the way he cupped my cheek and wiped my tears away in the police station. I don't think I will ever forget the words he said to me, "We're going to figure this out. No matter what."

I finally fall asleep, his words replaying over and over in my mind.

Chapter 32 ~ Chase

Chase's POV

It is a stare down, one that I wasn't going to back down from easily. Because I have nothing left to say. I already told them I didn't know where Brett was when they asked me all those weeks ago, but they were reluctant to accept my answer.

They think that if they wait long enough that I will crack.

That I will cave into the silence, afraid of the consequences if I don't respond.

They don't realise that I have nothing to hide, I don't know where he has been up until recently.

They, on the other hand, are currently having a hard time believing that.

The officer who had come to the dance earlier (who I had found out is named Dylan) is standing across from me next to Sage's dad. They are both crossing their arms over their chests, wearing deep scowls frowning down upon me, trying to seem intimidating as if they think they may be able to scare me into confessing. Sage left over five hours ago and I am still stuck here.

"I already told you. Up until recently when Brett found me I had no clue where he was or why he disappeared. I'm not lying! I don't know what else you want me to confess," I scowl back at them "Now I don't have any deep dark secrets that are nagging at me to be told, so unless you have something you need to get off your chests I suggest you move on to the next question," I state, gauging their reactions.

"Watch that tongue of your's son," Officer Dylan says, the frown on his face deepening.

"I have nothing left to say," I interject, crossing my arms over my chest.

"We have a witness saying that you helped plan the disappearance with Brett," Sage's dad says.

What the actual fuck?

Was this some sort of practical joke?

Was someone going to jump out from around the corner and scream "You just got punked?"

Because that's what it felt like to me.

A complete and utter practical joke.

Who the fuck told the police that I was involved from the start?

Who possibly wanted me to suffer?

My mind runs a blank and my head begins to thump aggressively. I scrunch my hands into fists, feeling the need to punch the closest thing. There is only one person who would possibly be psychotic enough to phone the fucking police just to see me suffer.

And that person is Aaron.

He took the photo. It must have been him. It had to be. He would have been the only one crazy enough to follow me outside that night. Take a photo, and then keep it.

This is what he meant when he said he would make me pay if I didn't show.

This Is my payment.

"Who?" I ask, wanting to confirm my suspicion.

"Someone who goes by the name of Aaron," Officer Dylan replies, looking from the files his hands to me.

Of course.

"Bring him in," I demand, anger coursing through my veins.

"You know we can't do that," Officer Dylan responds.

I'm beyond livid.

He played dirty, but he seems to be forgetting that I'm not the only one who has secrets that they don't want to be thrown out into the world. And if he thought I was going to play nice once I figured out that he was behind this, he had another thing coming.

Two can play this game.

I have three words running through my head at this current moment in time.

Bring.

It.

On.

"You want to know where that photo was taken?" I ask letting my eyes meet Sage's dad's square on.

"We already know that Chase. Aaron said that he saw the both of you heading towards the back of some old abandoned warehouse and that he recognised Brett. He decided to follow you both. And that is where the discussion became heated, so he took the photo and left. He said that you looked mad and dangerous," Officer Dylan is quick to respond.

That fucking liar.

If he is trying to take me down, make me pay, I will gladly return the favour.

I am going to make him suffer.

"He lied," I state. "Not about Brett and I talking but about the fact that it was just some old, warehouse. And that it was abandoned, another lie," I continue.

"What are you talking about?" Officer Dylan replies, leaning forward suddenly interested.

"That maybe you should get your facts straight before you come running after me and pointing the finger at me. That maybe you should have checked who you were receiving your information from," I retort.

"Aaron runs that warehouse, he is in charge of one of the largest illegal fighting organisations in the country," I say.

"How would you possibly know that?" Sage's dad pries.

"I worked for him. I became one of his best fighters and he offered for me to go pro. I declined. He wasn't happy, he wanted to show me off as one of his prized possessions, but I wasn't interested," I continue.

"I turned him down and didn't show up to fight when he wanted me to. He said I would regret it, and now I know why," I state anger burning deep within me. "Did you ever stop to question why you suddenly had that call? Why not weeks earlier when Brett first went missing? Didn't you ever stop to think? Why now?" I state keeping my voice level.

Before any of us in the room can move a police officer barges into the room, eyes wide and alarmed. He looks like he's seen a ghost. I take in his rugged expression and lift an eyebrow at him. What's got him so scared?

"Dylan, Mark, you need to come and see this right now!" he says clearly shaken.

"What is it, Matt?" Officer Dylan replies looking slightly confused at the sudden outburst.

"It's Brett Reed. He's here at the police station. He says he is here to clear Chase's name," The police officer stumbles out the words, and as he does my throat closes over.

Brett?

He was here?

Holy shit, what is going to happen now?

Chapter 33 ~ Sage

S age's POV

2 HOURS EARLIER

I wake to the buzzing of my phone. I look over at May who is still sound asleep.

I pick up my phone and look at the number. It seems oddly familiar so I answer.

"Hello?" I croak down the line.

"Hey Sage, it's Caleb." Suddenly a rush of memories from last night come flooding back to me as a sick feeling erupts in my gut. "I'm outside your friend's house. I need you to leave now.'"

"What? What are you talking about?" I whisper down the phone as I sit up.

"Look I'll explain everything, I promise. But you need to come out here now," he says urgently.

"Ok," I say, uncertain of what to do.

I decide to leave my dress and heels at May's house, I can get them later. I choose not to wake up May. I'll just send a text saying something came up. Maybe once all this shit has passed I can actually tell her what has happened.

I creep down the stairs to the front door, making sure I don't wake any of May's siblings in the process. I almost freak when I see the clock in the hallway that reads 4 am. I had only been asleep for 2 hours.

I quickly and silently open the door to find Caleb leaning against his car.

He looks me up and down, before frowning at my feet.

"You forgot shoes," he says, looking at me as if that's the most important thing right now.

"I only have heels and I just spent the whole night in them so no thank you," I say walking towards the car. "What's this all about?" I ask as a shiver runs through me due to the cool night breeze.

"Take a look for yourself," he says, moving from his position and opening the car door.

I almost choke at the sight of Brett Reed sitting in the passenger seat, now looking at me with clear recognition.

I look at Caleb, then at Brett and then at Caleb again.

"Do you know a place where we can all talk?" Caleb asks me.

"Uh, I'm guessing my house will be free. My dad's probably still at the station," I say, still in complete and utter shock.

"Cool, get in," Caleb says as he walks around to the driver's side.

I stand there for another second, unable to comprehend what's going on.

Why is Brett in the car? Why is Brett in Mapleville? What the hell is going on?

I quickly get in the car, unsure of what to say.

Caleb immediately starts the engine, "So have you guys formerly met?" he asks. He takes our silence as a no. "Sage, this is Brett. Brett, this is Sage."

Brett turns to me, his blonde hair looking like it hasn't been washed in weeks. The dark circles under his eyes make me think he hasn't been sleeping in weeks either. His brown eyes study me.

"You never told anyone," he says. I don't know whether it's a question or a statement but I immediately know what he is talking about.

Brett is referring to the day I saw him, which is now weeks ago. He begged me not to tell anyone his whereabouts.

"Only Chase," I say, my voice low.

Chase. Just speaking his name is enough to make my heart start beating overtime. I wonder if he's still at the police station. I hope he's alright.

"Wait, so you guys have met?" Caleb asks, sounding extremely confused.

"Not really," I say. "How do you know where I live?" I ask Caleb as he seems to know exactly where he is going.

"Had to find your address for Chase once," he shrugs. Right. This is the guy who Chase said can find anyone's address in Mapleville.

"Can someone please tell me what is going on?" I say growing impatient.

"Yes, I promise I will. As soon as we get inside," Caleb says, eyes focused on the road.

The rest of the ride is spent in silence. How am I even supposed to react in this kind of situation?

Caleb pulls up to my house and I rummage in my clutch for my keys. We all get out, myself leading the way followed by Caleb who is followed by Brett.

Thank god my father isn't back yet. It would be difficult explaining this to him.

My feet itch from walking on the overgrown grass taking residence on our once clear footpath. Another reminder of the lack of life living in this house.

I jam my keys through the door and turn on the lights as I enter the hallway. Brett and Caleb follow. I lead them to the dining table and sit down.

"Now will someone please explain to me what the fuck is going on?" I ask frustrated.

I had ruined my father and I's relationship and the guy I like is currently being interrogated. The life couldn't get any worse at this point.

"After I dropped you off last night I went home and found this dude at my door," he says nudging his head in Brett's direction. I can't read the emotions on Brett's face. All I can see is exhaustion.

"You can probably imagine I freaked the fuck out! What the hell was Brett Reed doing at my door, you know?" Caleb says. "I personally try to steer clear of all Mapleville's drama but nope the Universe just wants to drag me into the biggest scandal this town has ever had."

"Details please Caleb," I say impatiently. I feel Brett's gaze on me as if he is trying to work me out.

"I'll explain," Brett interjects as if he knows that if Caleb tells the story it will go on forever. "Last night I was at some pub miles away. I heard on the news that a suspect had been taken in for further questioning after new evidence was discovered. The only suspect the police are even considering is Chase. I know he has no role in this. Nobody has a fucking role in this but me. So I'm going to turn myself in."

"I knew Chase was innocent but nobody listened to me. Everyone in this town just likes to believe whatever sounds best. They don't care about the facts," I say, staring at the table.

"They are a thing by the way," Caleb says to Brett, referring to Chase and I. Brett doesn't even look surprised.

I ignore his comment. "Why now? Why not ages ago?" I ask Brett. There better be a good reason for this.

"I couldn't live the life I was being forced to live. My parents are nuts. They want me to be some perfect kid to keep up with their perfect reputation. But I don't want to be the perfect kid. Everything that seems perfect is actually so broken inside. Just like them," he says bitterly. I had heard Chase talk the same way about Brett's family. About Brett himself.

"I never intended on coming back. The aim was to get as far away from here as possible. As far away from them as possible. But when I heard Chase was being dragged into my shit when he was innocent I couldn't live with the guilt. I hoped it would just fade away, but it hasn't. So here I am," he says, voice completely emotionless. It is evident to see that he is so broken mentally, and currently, he looks broken physically too.

"Hey what about that fight you and Chase had?" Caleb asks. Chase had mentioned it before but only briefly.

"Just family shit," Brett says. He looks at me to gauge my reaction, wondering if I know what he is implying. I do. The fight must have been about the affair between Brett's mother and Chase's dad.

"How'd you do it?" I ask curiously. "How have you survived for this long? You left no evidence whatsoever. You didn't even take your phone."

"I took enough food and money for three days," he states. "There's always food in my cupboards at home. My parents were always too busy fine-dining to have noticed what was missing. I took a jacket and the clothes on my back. That's all I needed until I got to the next town, then I had connections to people, and I went from there."

"Didn't they know who you were?" Caleb asks confused.

"Some did. Some didn't. I just explained my reasons to those who did and they promised not to say anything if I only stayed one night," he shrugs.

"Why did you come back to Mapleville the other night? When you saw Chase at the fight?" I ask.

"I just had a feeling. I knew he would probably turn back to fighting after everything that has happened. I went there with no idea whether he would be fighting there that night or not. But he was there. As soon as he saw me I regretted my decision. I tried to leave but he followed me. You probably know what happened afterwards," he says not wanting to explain more than he has to. I nod.

That had been the night Chase had turned up at my house, bruised and injured. The night our lips had met and night I knew there was no escaping the feelings I got whenever he was around. My head aches just thinking about it. I just want to be with him right now.

"Now we get to why you're here Sage. Obviously apart from you and Chase's relationship and the fact that you were dragged into the police station last night too..." Caleb says but Brett interrupts.

"Why did you get called into the police station?" He asks suddenly confused.

"Because I wasn't going to let Chase take the fall for knowing your whereabouts when I had too at one point," I say giving a shrug.

Caleb just smirks at me, "How adorable," I give him the rude finger in response. "Anyways we need you to call the police station. Tell them Brett is on his way."

"Why couldn't you just call?" I ask.

"You're the daughter of the head detective, you have power," he says. Any power I had faded as soon as I opened my mouth last night. "Besides I knew Chase would kill me if I didn't keep you in the loop."

I just nod and take out my phone. Here goes nothing.

~~~~~~~~~~~~~~~~~~~~~~~~~~~~~~~~~

☆ Please vote and comment ☆
~~~~~~~~~~~~~~~~~~~~~~~~~~~~~~~~~

Chapter 34 ~ Chase

C hase's POV

I blink and give my head a small shake hoping to refocus my mind onto what is happening around me, but currently that is complete and utter chaos.

Brett has arrived, and suddenly no one knows what to do.

The town's police station has gone into meltdown mode and I am sitting here rooted to the spot, not knowing what to do. It feels like the calm before the storm and I am not sure if I am ready to walk through these doors and face the colossal drama that is happening on the other side.

The sound of someone walking through the door stopping a mere metre away from me catches my diverted attention almost immediately and I quickly drift my eyes onto their face and run my eyes along their features. The guy presented in front of me holds an aura that oozes confidence, and he holds himself firm and strong.

"You're free to go, son, Brett's appearance has cleared everything up," he says. I snap my eyes to his.

Is he serious? This is all actually over? I'm free?

Free, the word feels weird to think about now, after everything that has happened over the past few months. It was a weird thing, freedom. Lately, I didn't feel like the word held much value to me anymore.

Brett truly came back and showed, despite the wrath that will most likely be waiting for him at home.

My stomach feels uneasy thinking about his parent's reaction to his return.

I stand and my body aches, a spark of pain ignites in my feet and runs its way up my legs like a vine. I realise that I have been sitting in this chair for the past few hours, unmoving and numb.

One thought is fuelling my movements currently, and that is the fact that I am going to find Sage, and finally get that kiss.

I walk past the officer and into the hallway, absorbing the fact that the commotion has died down since when I had zoned out last. I turn my head quickly, wondering if Brett is actually here. I make my way down the hallway and I notice Brett's voice before I actually see him.

I turn the corner and see that Brett is making his way towards me with two officers walking behind him, keeping within distance to grab him if needed. They appear to be steering him in the direction of another room near the one I have just come from.

My eyes scan over him, absorbing his mop of blonde shaggy hair which looks dishevelled and messy. I let my eyes travel along his face before stopping on his eyes, which are already locked on me. His earthy brown eyes look tired but upon seeing me they brighten the slightest.

"Chase," Brett says coming up and stopping short less than a meter away.

"Why did you do it? why did you come back?" I ask my mind a mess.

"I wasn't about to let you take the blame for something that was my problem, you did that enough when we were younger," He states.

"What about your parents?" I question, knowing the crap he will receive for his sudden disappearing act.

"It's ok, I'll figure it out," he replies keeping his tone low.

The silence that engulfs the narrow hallway becomes uncomfortable and I shift my footing from one side to the other.

"Thanks," I say my green eyes flashing to his.

"I said I would fix it, I wasn't lying Chase," he responds. I don't know how to respond. I don't know what else to say.

"Chase, you might want to hurry, your girl is outside waiting for you," Brett says before the police officers shove his shoulders edging him to keep moving.

And those are the only words that it takes for me to turn and rush towards the doors. As I make my way there I notice that Sage's dad is standing off to the side of the room. His eyes meet mine as he makes his way up to me, giving me a grim look.

"Look after her," He grumbles, mustering his best glare.

"I intend to Mr Hill, I always have," I reply before turning and making my way towards the exit.

I jog until I'm just outside the doors, and let my eyes run along the parking lot, my eyes searching for Sage.

My eyes meet her electric blue ones making my heart stop in my chest. I make my way over to her, as she leans against Caleb's car. I let my eyes meet his cold grey ones, and he gives me a small nod, and I give him one in return. I don't let my eyes linger on his for too long before they meet Sages'.

I can't help the feeling that begins in my stomach, as a small smile graces her features.

"Hey," she mumbles, looking up at me. I don't waste a second before I grab her waist and pull her to my chest, wrapping my arms around her holding her to me.

"Hi," I reply taking in her delicate smell of roses, as I let it consume my senses. And I let out a sigh of relief, god I missed that smell.

"You're free," she says her smile widening as her eyes look over my face and I do the same.

A small frown tugs at the corner of my mouth as I look at the bags under her eyes, I reach my hand up and run my finger under her eyes

"Did you not sleep at all last night? Miss me so much you couldn't even sleep?" I ask trying to lighten the mood.

"Oh, shut up," she mumbles into my chest before giving my shoulder a light shove.

"As adorable as this whole Romeo and Juliet thing you guys have got going on is, I would seriously like to eat breakfast sometime this morning," Caleb's voice interjects.

"Shut it Caleb," I growl out, tightening my hold on Sage not wanting to let her go yet.

"Okay, Okay. Jeez calm down bro," Caleb teases as he makes his way to the driver's seat. "I'll be in the car when you finally decide to join me you two lovebirds," he calls over his shoulder before slipping into the car and out of view.

"Chase?" Sage asks lifting her head, letting her captivating eyes meet mine.

"Yes sweetheart," I reply.

"We should probably get in the car, knowing Caleb he will drive off and leave us here if we don't hurry up," She says with a light laugh.

She begins to turn and make her way towards the car. But before she can take another step, I grab her wrist and pull her back to me.

She looks up at me slightly stunned. "Chase?" she questions "What are you doing?" she asks.

"I promised myself if it worked out, that I would do one thing to celebrate," I say looking down at her.

"What?" she asks clearly confused.

"This," I say, and with that I lean my head down and capture her lips with mine, catching her completely off guard. She stands motionless and completely stunned before she lightly responds pressing her lips gently against mine, causing sparks to erupt making my head spin.

She lightly pulls away looking up at me.

"I bet you didn't think you would end up falling for the suspect now did you?" I ask smirking down at her.

"Who says I've fallen for you?" she asks feigning fake confusion, and with that, she sends me a wink over her shoulder before she turns and pulls me towards the car.

This girl truly is something else.